Around the Table

An Anthology

Veterans' Voices Writing Workshop

WORKSHOP FACILITATED BY JACK CARMAN

COVER DESIGN BY LOREN CHRISTOFFERSON

COVER PHOTOGRAPH BY VICTORIA STAUFFENBERG FOR THE
NATIONAL PARK SERVICE

Table of Contents

3

4

Introduction

The Veterans' Voices Writing Workshop, a project of Arts and Culture El Dorado, is a free writing workshop that is open to all veterans from any branch of service. In the ten years since its founding, the Workshop has offered El Dorado County veterans a supportive, stimulating environment in which to hone their craft, to express and challenge themselves, and to find their voice. In those ten years, in evening meetings around a table in the Veterans Memorial Building, as discussions, critiques, and laughter filled the room while coffee cups stained rings into rough drafts, the Workshop has also forged lasting bonds between its participants, giving them cherished memories and a sense of community.

Seven anthologies of writing from the Workshop have been produced. This is the first that does not feature a piece by Will Martin, who passed away late last year. A longtime, beloved Workshop participant, Will's introspective, sharply observed accounts of life before, during, and after his service in the military— sometimes acerbic, sometimes tender, but almost always funny—are sorely missed in the pages of this anthology, just as he is missed by those who survive him.

This anthology is dedicated to Will. It contains several tributes to him, including one from his wife, Dora. Its cover image, the Vietnam Veterans Memorial, and its title, "Around the Table", were selected by Workshop participants to honor Will and to celebrate the camaraderie they have found through the Veterans' Voices Writing Workshop.

We are grateful to Jack Carman, a longtime educator and writing instructor, for facilitating these workshops; to the Veterans Memorial Building, where workshops are held; and to the County of El Dorado, through its Veterans Affairs Commission, whose funding makes this anthology possible. The California Arts Council also supports this program through an operations grant. To our other supporters, and especially to our readers: Thank you for supporting El Dorado County Veterans.

Willard (Will) Albert Martin Jr.

1944 – 2023

WILL MARTIN was born Willard Albert Martin Jr. in San Jose, CA, two months before his dad left for the Pacific Theater during WWII. Will lived in a 300-square-foot wooden shack on his grandparents' dairy farm. His family moved into a tract home development in January 1949.

He tried to enlist in the US Marine Corps after graduating high school at seventeen but was temporarily classified 4F until the orthodontist removed his braces.

He enlisted in the Air Force in October 1962. He trained as an Air Policeman and was stationed with the Strategic Air Command at Little Rock AFB, AK, and Ramey AFB, Puerto Rico.

Will married Dora Virginia Alvarez in June 1968 and was hired by the San Jose Police Department on September 11th that same year. Before graduating from San Jose State University in 1975, Will and Dora had three children.

Contributors

MIKE DURANT was drafted into the Army in 1966. He served in Vietnam in 1967-68 with the 1st Signal Brigade in Phu Bai, I Corps. He was attached to the Army Security Agency in a secure compound surrounded by US Marines. He describes his duty: "I was safe in the rear with the gear." Mike was born and grew up in Sacramento, where he graduated from Cal State University Sacramento and received a Masters of Journalism from UCLA. After graduation he worked with a series of small California newspapers. From 1991 to 1997, he served as the Pacific Editor for Stars and Stripes in Tokyo. On his return to the U.S., Mike worked three years for the Stockton Record newspaper as a copy editor before taking a position with the California Department of Water Resources as a technical writer/editor. He retired in 2011, and now lives in El Dorado Hills, California. Mike has five grandchildren. To keep busy, he skis and swims and volunteers as a docent at the Effie Yeaw Nature Center in Carmichael, California.

WILLIAM BLAYLOCK is the author of *Invisible: PTSD's Stealth Attack on a Vietnam War Veteran* (available on Amazon and wherever books are sold). Northern California Publishers and Authors published him in their 2015 Anthology.

He is a Vietnam Army combat veteran. While serving from March 1968 to March 1969, he was attached to the 3rd Marine Division.

Over the following 35 years, after his military discharge, he had 36 different jobs. Although he kept busy with his marriage, children, and work, he was always on edge, and unable to find peace.

"With the help of a friend, I went to a Vet Center and started my healing process. My wife and children deserve credit for loving me enough to stay when I was at my worst. Writing has been my greatest therapy. Now my days are filled with sharing this therapeutic outlet with veterans and active duty military. My prayer is that they will not wait 35 years to realize the effects that military trauma may have put on them."

PATRICK McCANN served in the US Navy as an Electronic Warfare Technician on the USS *McClusky* (FFG-41). After his service, he got married and had two kids. As a stay-at-home dad, he raised and homeschooled his two girls in Rescue, CA.

He attended DeVry University and graduated with a Bachelor's Degree in Computer Information Systems in 2017.

He currently resides in Placerville, CA.

TIM WHALEN was born and raised in Wells, MN, and graduated high school in 1984. He immediately joined the US Navy, and honorably served aboard four ships and four shore duty stations as a Torpedoman's Mate, performing a variety of collateral duties (as a Drug & Alcohol Program Advisor, a Career Counselor, a Leadership Academy Instructor, and in other positions) from July 1984 to September 2006.

He attended Columbia College, graduating with an AS degree in Criminal Justice Administration. Upon retirement from the Navy, he briefly worked as a Transition Service Officer with Disabled American Veterans, and then for 4+ years for the State of California Employment Development Department as a Veterans' Employment Specialist.

Tim started as the Office Manager at the Citrus Heights Vet Center in October 2011 and was promoted to Outreach Coordinator in June 2015.

He has two children and lives with his wife and family in Placerville, CA.

PETE LA COMBE was born in Boulder, CO, on January 28, 1949.

Shortly after this, his family moved to Torrance, CA, a suburb just south of downtown Los Angeles. He graduated from Carson High School in Torrance in 1967.

When not in school—and sometimes when he should have been—he could have been found paddling his surfboard into the Pacific Ocean, looking to catch the wave of his life.

After high school, Pete worked as an electrician's helper at the Todd Shipyard in San Pedro, CA, for a year.

On September 22, 1968, he joined the US Army, and the next day found himself at Fort Ord, CA, where he was assigned to B51—a basic training unit—where he was made a squad leader.

After graduating from basic training, he was marched down the street to Company A12 for AIT (Advanced Infantry Training) as a mortarman.

Four months later he was in Vietnam, assigned to Delta Troop--1st Cavalry Division, 9th Cavalry Division—in which he served as a gunner on an 81mm mortar squad.

TRAVIS L. DOVER served three years as a Specialist of the U.S. Army, 3rd Stryker Brigade, 2nd Infantry Division, 1/14 Cavalry. One of those years was in Iraq. "I have been married to my wonderful wife for thirteen years and share with her six children and counting: five girls and an often sticky and naked toddler boy. I am grateful to Bill Blaylock of Veterans' Voices who invited me to participate and share some of my writing. I enjoy being in the company of the members of Veterans' Voices as they have life experiences and wisdom that they share that can help me become a better writer."

RICHARD WEAVER was born and raised in Southeast Idaho. After graduating high school, he attended junior college for two semesters, then attended college in Utah. He enlisted in the US Army in 1960. He attended basic training at Fort Ord, California. He then attended medical corpsman training at Fort Sam, Houston, Texas. He was assigned to the US Army Hospital, West Point, NY. His enlistment ended with him achieving the rank of E-6 and NCIOC of the Eye, Ear, Nose, and Throat clinic in the hospital.

After his tour of duty, he worked in law enforcement for 37 years, followed by a 14-year career in Human Resources with a Native American tribe. He married his wife of 58 years a few months after being discharged from the Army. They have eight children together.

RALPH MONTEROSA entered the military in December 1968. He completed two years of ROTC training at Midwestern University, but decided to pass on signing a contract, as he had recently gotten

9

married and was a full-time student. He became a mechanic at a reserve unit in Jersey City, New Jersey, before being ordered to active duty in January 1970. After basic training, he completed Engineer School at Fort Belvoir, Virginia.

Ralph served the next six years as a Platoon Sergeant with the 469th Engineer Battalion. He served an additional four years with a Cadre Unit, as a part of a pre-inspection team.

Tribute to Will Martin
Mike Durant

I'll miss Will Martin. He was not only a fun writing comrade, but a personal friend. We enjoyed some great laughs too, during and from our meetings in Placerville each Monday evening. He was a cornerstone of our motley writing group. With his experience as a former San Jose cop and Air Force veteran, Will brought a fun perspective to our discussions about storytelling. He blended humor with a touch of self-deprecation that endeared him to us all. He had a knack for finding humor in his own foibles and quirks. His wit was sharp, his observations keen, but never at the expense of others. Instead, he turned the spotlight inward, sharing moments of vulnerability with a disarming honesty. Will's authentic humor was refreshing. I think about him often. Those memories make me smile. Thanks, Will.

Willard Albert Martin Jr.
William Blaylock

Christian, Airman, Police Officer, Knight of Columbus, All around Good Guy and My Friend!

I met Will when working at DST Output in El Dorado Hills. Like most workplace acquaintances, ours started with casual conversation in the break room. We discovered some similarities: we had both served the City of San Jose in the Police Department; we had played the clarinet in high school; and we had taken flying lessons.

In May 2006, my wife and I were taking a trip and leaving from San Francisco. The night before we left, we stayed at the El Rancho Hotel in San Bruno. They let you leave your car for free while you're gone. The next morning, Betty and I were in the guest lounge having a packaged pastry and coffee. While waiting for the airport shuttle, another couple came in to get their coffee and pastry. I looked up and although they were facing away from me, the guy looked like my friend from work. Will always stood straight and tall and did not let his stomach reach over his belt; something I, and most men our age, do not manage very well. I say, "Will?" He saw me and we started laughing.

We made the appropriate introductions and explained to our wives how we knew each other. Will and Dora were going to Italy and Betty and I to Spain. Our shuttle arrived, so we made plans to meet for coffee or dinner after our return.

Both our wives are of Hispanic heritage. Will understood a little Spanish and would watch Spanish tele-novellas with Dora. I think he only watched to look at the beautiful women.

Over the years, we developed a strong bond of respect and mutual esteem. Will was a kind and thoughtful man, only thinking of other people and their likes and needs. He rarely accepted an offer of help for himself, but he was always there to help others. Will took part and assisted with the projects and needs of our church and the Knights of Columbus. As a member of The Knights of Columbus, Will attained the highest level of fourth degree.

I attended and volunteered to work security at the Reno Air Races for many years, and invited Will to go with me. He says, "I'm still working, but as soon as I retire, I'd like to go." Will kept his word. We only missed one year, due to my poor planning. My wife and I took a trip East to see the fall colors. The Air Races are the first week of September, which, of course, is when the trees start to change and show their splendid fall colors. Oops, my bad! Sorry, Will.

Will and I volunteered to work Air Race security. We stayed at a hotel and worked Thursday through Sunday. Will would tell people that when in Reno, we slept together, which embarrassed the heck out of me, so I was quick to explain: not in the same bed! He got a big kick out of that joke. When COVID-19 stopped the world, that was the last of our Reno Air Race adventures; rich food, steaks, pasta, and desserts ... Oh yeah, and airplanes, too. I know some of you won't believe this, but while away, without our wives, Will didn't drink all *that* much red wine!

Two years ago this December, Will wanted to start a bible study with Ralph Monterosa and me. A couple of times, we met at Ralph's or my home, but mostly I remember going to Will and Dora's; it was easier for him at home due to requiring oxygen. Each time, Ralph and I told Dora that we'd bring our lunches, but you all know how generous and providing Dora is, and she would make something or go out and buy Togo's or other lunches for us. As an aside, no matter how much Will and I insisted we did not need dessert, Ralph always brought a whole or half apple pie from Ruthann's kitchen or a bakery. Don't tell anyone, but we'd split it three ways and dispose of the evidence. We always read and discussed some scripture, though often talking with food in our mouths.

For those of you who knew Will, there is nothing more I can say. For those of you who did not, there is so much more.

I am so very proud of my friend's desire and effort to complete the writing of his memoir. Writing a book is an arduous task, and even though Will was sick and not feeling well, he did it. Good job, Buddy.

I can't end my tribute without reminding you of Will's story about the pig. Everyone loves that story.

Our good times will remain in my heart, my friend. Thank you, Will.

I miss you.

A Letter for Will
Dora Martin

Dear Members of Veterans' Voices Writing Workshop,

I met Will in San Jose in December of 1966, one week after he proudly had served 4 years in the U.S. Air Force. I think he had been "celebrating for a week" and I didn't even think he would remember meeting me. Soon after we were married, the San Jose Police Department hired him as a full-pledged rookie. He never brought his work home and only told me about humorous escapades while on duty. In 1984, he left the department as a respected and seasoned officer who had seen more than he wanted to remember to work for IBM. All those years he had continued to go to school, managing to earn a college and a master's degree, often working two and three jobs while being a great husband and father to our three children.

In 1994, we moved to El Dorado County and, gradually, through the years, began accumulating new friends, amongst them Bill Blaylock, one of the founders of the veterans' writing group. Will had always considered himself very limited in his writing expression and usually avoided having to write school papers, so when Bill encouraged Will to connect with this unique project, Will became very excited and motivated to join this innovative group of writers who had served their country with valor and courage. He always looked forward to being at every meeting and was disappointed when he had to miss one. To Will's amazement and mine, Will found a strong voice through his words on paper. He became a story writer under the inspiration of Weston De Walt, Mike Restaino, and Jack Carman, and with the help of amazing other veterans. He was first published in the 2018 Anthology and later in 3 others. After all those years in school, and with so many untold stories of what he had seen while a police officer, he felt the true therapy and joy of writing.

15

Will spent the last months of his life writing his stories for his family and sharing his life experiences. He learned he had many other things he still wanted to write about, especially for the next anthology. He struggled with not being able to attend meetings due to his illness but was so proud of having been a part of this special project. Through his writing, I got to know Will in a way that made me so grateful for his service to his country and the community he served as a police officer.

Will would be so proud that you have honored him with this dedication in the next anthology. His family and I are so appreciative and look forward to seeing his name appear in one more anthology. I hope that other veterans will be encouraged by this project to also find their writer's voice, as it has such amazing healing powers.

With love and respect, Dora Martin

The Dance of Uncertainty
Pat McCann

In the rhythm of life's symphony,
We navigate through strife and harmony,
A stranger's hand we gently take,
Our hearts, the canvas, for love to make.

Will you be the light that guides my way,
Or will you cast shadows for more doubts to sway?
To understand the self through another's eyes,
The connection and feelings help solidify.

Through chaos and uncertainty, we find,
In time, we reshape the key to our mind,
Boundaries we discover, some we'll break,
Our minds and hearts, are a constant remake.

For every role we play, we'll be,
A range from hero to hellion, you'll see,
But let me know if I'm a blessing or the worst,
Will our existential bubble continue to increase or burst?

So, let's dance through this uncertainty,
And find the beauty in our rarity,
Footfalls rhythmically stepping in time together,
Moving through space claiming the next moment called forever.

The Lies of the Wolves
Pat McCann

Seeing was believing, but now, the light of gas (gaslighting) illuminates our sight.

Belief, once perceived as pure, is now obscured and has morphed into the next lie by skillful illusion's might. Untruths sold on repeat slip past our mental defenses. If you are one of the perpetually unaware, their hold is hard or impossible to dispel. Those who bend reality repeatedly risk its breaking. Their impositions will be done and enforced, over and over without considering the costs or consequences.

The wolf hunting the village forgets his howl and uses a new tactic, exclaiming "Wolf!", for they will get conditioned to it and quickly learn to ignore the warning. The critical mind given to most is designed to question. Those that do this suffer from those who refuse to employ their mental gifts. Fools and their handlers force fallacy as gospel, dumbing down the masses, influencing perception, and making the collective step, one that is in reverse.

Subscribing to tribal or mob groupthink is a shortcut, but it may not serve your best interest; be cautious about whom you follow. Calamity calls the lemmings, especially when they follow too close to those unaware or ignoring the path ahead, over the cliff. Consider who you let lead you, for they may not have your heart in tow.

We live in a time when emotional arguments have gained the ability to trump intellect and logic. Depth and substance, in thought, seem to have been relegated to a fad of the past. Media, including the "social" version and its engineering, have already divided the masses well. So many are traumatized by so many lies that they are quite ready with a hair trigger to reject that which doesn't comply with the narrative that they have been sold. I fear our human experiment will end in disarray without the wisdom to see us through the day. I pray that you prove me wrong!

Our Democracy
Pete La Combe

I never paid too much attention to politics. As a kid, I remember my parents watching something called "Gallup poll". What the hell was that? People galloping around a pole. I got on my bike and pedaled to the beach. *What a waste of time,* I thought. *I can't vote anyways.* The next time I thought about our government was in high school. Our country, it was said, was the best, and I agreed, even after that shitcan war in Viet Nam. After I made it home from Nam, I found out it was a political war between Communism and Democracy in South East Asia. While on patrol in Nam, I talked many hours to many Vietnamese Coke Girls (beautiful tiny young girls selling ice cold Cokes on Hondas). We talked many times trying to understand this fucking insane war. They all agreed it was insane, every fucking one of them, all with a teary eye.

"GI go home no sweat Democracy same-same as Communism. Communist party same-same as Democratic party. It works here. We have good leaders. You can't protect us from communism. We are a communist country. We can't change you. You can't change us."

Why we fight, kill and destroy makes no sense, except for us pawns of war to try to stay alive, or the country's need to feed their political war machines, till they finally blow up the world in their prediction of the end, in a man-made religious rapture. Are we just going up in the sky like smoke?

I took Political Science at Long Beach City College, from Congressman Mark Hannaford, former Mayor of Lakewood in the mid '70s. PACs (Political Action Committees) should be illegal, he felt: it was legal bribery, it's buying votes, etc. It's all about winning. Mudslinging liars win. Republican or Democrat, whether it makes sense to or not, nowadays they don't fight fair. Divide and conquer the people: it worked in the past. I hope what I am seeing now doesn't get worse. You can't change history, but winners can try. Calling us men serving in Nam 'baby killers', that hurt. It's a bit ironic to me, when millions of women decide to kill their own. Look

19

in the mirror, all you name-calling, delusional people, then tell me what you see.

The world would be a better place if we put a world bounty on insane leaders like Putin, and somehow get demonic religious leaders to end their warlike feuds that never end, opting instead for never-ending peace. Peace for a change. See the smoke and ashes and the dead in the wake of your bullshit religious feuds? Peace worldwide could flourish. Will our country turn in on itself over hate, or will it grow together and try learning from the past?

Day of the Pervert
Pete La Combe

I still remember holding that bowstring that day, shaking and trembling, aiming at that sick FLICKER's penis, now back in his pants, walking toward me slow, with a grin, telling me to get in his turquois and white '57 Chevy. As I backed away, I was scared shitless. Thinking back at times, I wish the bowstring had slipped, sending the arrow straight through his penis, nuts, and femoral artery, like a shish kebab. I know it sounds harsh, but you weren't there seeing the sick, crazy, insane face staring back—the face which would come to haunt my childhood nightmares. I sensed, from the fury written on his face, that I wasn't the first kid he tried to kidnap, but that I was the only one that had gotten away. (He thought he had me.) If I didn't have my bow and arrow that day, I wouldn't be here. That stare of insane fury, looking me in the eye, still haunts me to this day. The thought that he's done it before popped into my head who knows how many times after. I found out years later that a serial killer was on the loose in Los Angeles in the late '50s early '60s, who was never caught. I saw the devil in human form that day. Could it be him?

If I had it to do over, I am sure after what I know now and have seen in Viet Nam that the best of the best die for no good reason. What if I did my good deed of the day like a good Boy Scout, shooting him and watching him bleed out, riding my bike to the Police Station to tell my story to the cops? I think maybe I would get a merit badge. Maybe get on TV for being the youngest kid to shoot and take down a kidnapping, kid-killing pervert. What if? Sounds cool to me.

Freddy
Pete La Combe

I remember Freddy. He always wanted to hang out with the older kids in the neighborhood. He could hardly wait to turn eleven, when he could join the boy scouts, having heard about summer camp up in Lake Arrowhead, where kids rode horses, hiked, and slept in tents. He didn't believe how cold the water was in 'Deep Creek' if you tried to swim to the bottom, down into the darkness. I bet him: "The creek's so deep, you can't touch bottom."

I didn't tell him that it's pitch-black, ear-popping, brain-freezing cold, and scary as hell. When nobody in troop #241 could meet the challenge, we had to stop Freddy from trying before he almost froze. He was the youngest in our troop, and we couldn't keep up with him—he was always going for it. He was the undisputed champ in selling donuts to buy new tents. I thought I was doing good selling eleven dozen, but I didn't have a chance against Freddy's eighty-one dozen and his huge smile and sales pitch that Barnum and Bailey would be proud of. He was fun to watch in action.

As he got older, he learned to dance like James Brown, got a fake ID at 15, and won most dance contests at the "Grand", a converted old theater and now a dance hall. He was so pissed off when they found out he wasn't 18 and got banned. He was a slim five-foot-tall golden-glove champ when we got back in touch after I got out of the Army in February, '70. I never forgot the day two sheriffs told us, "You gotta go! Stop fighting on the sand by Hermosa Pier!" They said we were causing a disturbance.

What, a little guy slapping the crap out of somebody taller? It bothers them that I am slow, that he's teaching me to block. Both of us laughed.

Figure it out somewhere else, guys, maybe your backyard? But not here.

For months Freddy stopped by (I never knew where he lived; he was over just about every day at first). He wanted to hear all the war stories about my year in Viet Nam that I could remember, until I had no more. He would tell me if I was repeating myself.

Not knowing where he lived, I lost contact. It seemed to me that not being able to serve his country, for some reason, left a hole. He said he wished could have gone. I told him he didn't miss anything good, except coming home.

A few years had gone by when I stopped by my old Scout Master's house, Joe Wilson, for a visit. Before I knew it, he said, "Did you hear what happened to Freddy?"

"No," I replied.

"He committed suicide."

"What!"

"He left a note that said 'Viet Nam messed his head up.'"

"He never went, Joe."

"I know."

The Look
Ralph Monterosa

It was eight o'clock in the morning and already there was a hot, hazy sun burning down on us. There wasn't the slightest chance of a cloud to offer respite from the heat, baking our dry leather-like skin, hot to the touch. Across the field, only a grayish cloud rose up from the parched earth. All color was gone from the land. No "Sky Blue or Sunshine Bright" that brings the land back to life. The entire farm was a wilted grey. Every so often the remnants of a dead stalk had broken through the soil and stood lifeless.

No time. I quickly turned back to the task in front of us. We were loading up the same old truck we had used on the farm to carry goods to the market. It sat for a long time without need of use. Three years with very little but dry death.

Time to escape this hellish desert. We were loading all the belongings we could carry for our long journey west. The old Packard was already full with personals, and enough room for Jeremy, my sixteen-year-old son, and my wife and two daughters. The rest of the boys would climb in the truck with me. How could such an ungodly tragedy come upon us as a plague from the heavens?

The farm had been in the family five generations, since the land rush. Now we were just walking away, as the bank now owned this worthless land. The equipment had been sold at a bank auction, for pennies on the dollar. There was nothing left to do but leave for what he had prayed was a better life. But it was still grave sorrow. All we could do was walk away. We were too sad, but we had shed all our tears already.

Now it was almost mechanical as we loaded the truck with what we might need or be able to use. There were so many memories and treasures which must be left behind.

Everyone knew what they must do, and were moving as if in a slow-motion parade. Again I thought, "How could this happen?" Every so often, one of the children would stop and just stare across the barren land. It looked like waves of dried-up ash. It was an ocean of dry waves.

24

Now there was no time to stop. There were two reasons we needed to keep loading. To get our minds off of leaving everything we had ever known, and the finality of the process. As much as we saw it coming, we could never be ready for this. We always held out hope. But now it was too painful to linger.

Whenever I caught anyone fall into this trance-like stare, I would give them what the children referred to as "The Look." When I was wearing the look, everyone miraculously became enlightened to the task at hand. It often provoked the sharing of smiles. Not today. It did, however, keep everyone in motion and back at the tearful task.

I'm not sure where this erroneous, provocative, sometimes enlightening, benign tool came from. I remember my father using it to get our attention. I guess it was passed along from generation to generation. It was only used infrequently, as to not lose the seriousness of its effect. It was far more effective than any well-chosen words. It provoked a well delivered message that almost always got the desired response. Jeremy was on the receiving end at the moment, and the response was mechanical. Mother's rocker was passed up to me in one quick motion. The surrounding scenery had been put on hold for the present. Back to the task at hand.

Every so often, Mother and I would have a momentary look at each other. Without saying a word, we had a clear vision of each other's thoughts. The pain in our eyes said it all.

How do we turn this sorrowful moment of the past into an excited vision of the future? I needed to force a smile for the future. O.K., time to break the silence. Even if it was just pointing out the next thing to load with an excited "Load Happy Voice". We have to break that slow-motion, zombie-like look. Every so often, I would announce how helpful a piece of farm or kitchen equipment would be in California. That was quite a stretch, but it seemed to be working. Was everyone just acting this out as I was, or was the excitement growing? They were planting visions of things they had never seen and were yet to come.

Everyone was now in quick step, with a bounce to follow. In reality, anything had to be better than what we were leaving behind. We would be on our way to California. My brother had made this

25

trip 17 years prior. He would give us a portion of his large land to pick up and farm. That portion had not been farmed before and would need a lot of work. Perfect. I needed this. For the children, a life of options would be offered, beyond anything they had here. This is the discussion that filled the air as frowns turned to real or forced smiles. No matter the circumstance, anything was better than this.

We were done packing and ready to start our adventure. We all stood ground, waiting to get in the car and truck. I said, "Let's go." But no one moved. In an act of desperation, I gave them "The Look". Instant movement accompanied and chatter broke the silence. We were on our way. Sorrow seemed to turn to joy. Even Mom moved with a renewed bounce in her step and a smile on her face. She was smart and picked up on the event. Everyone followed. We were all together on this one.

Fears of the Unknown
William Blaylock

Fearing the unknown; what a terrifying thought to consider. But everything in the future is unknown and likely fearful. Being afraid of the future is called anxiety. Worry or fear of things that have not yet happened will beat a person down. I have seen anxiety's influence on people. Though being concerned and therefore making plans is, or ought to be, a part of responsible adulthood living. Short of being physically or mentally incapacitated, everyone needs to plan for their unknown fears of the future. For those who do not have the capacity or ability, it is then up to the rest of us, who are competent, to step in and assist those unqualified. The influence of this action is called Community. What a glorious concept. (Even airlines promote community in their emergency plan: "Help others, after you have secured your own oxygen mask.") I.e., take care of yourself first, then help others.

Make your plans. Consider your options. Are your choices safe for your future unknowns? Realistic? What are possible ramifications of your plans? If your plan is safe for you, does or will it hurt another's?

I have lived my life as reactionary. My wife and I have made plans in reaction to, or for coping with, things that often happen in life. We are physically and financially sound. I can respond to potential threats, and am comfortable with our plans to weather the unknown fears of the future.

I will take this opportunity to offer a brief political rant. We must not depend on our government to save us from our own poor decisions and irresponsible behavior. Our government has enough trouble being responsible for itself, let alone reckless, unproductive drags on society. In the words of Mark Twain, "Never put off till tomorrow what can be put off till day-after-tomorrow just as well." No. Wait, that wasn't it. What he said was, "The older I get, the more clearly I remember things that never happened." No, no, not that one either. Aah, never mind what Mark Twain said. What I say is, "Be responsible for yourself."

As I continued to reflect on this subject, I came up with a truly fearful thought. Fear of the truth, our own truth! It is not unknown; the fact is, it is extremely well known.

I am certain that there is no person, alive or dead (except for two, Jesus and Mary), that does not or did not have a fear of the truth being known. These fears are because of our past. Law enforcement Investigators encourage suspects to confess to their crimes. Telling them, "The truth will set you free." Confessors, i.e., priests, in the Catholic church and perhaps other religions, encourage their laity to confess the truth. But for the person sheltering their truth, even after being forgiven of their sins, they still do not want their truths made known to others. Though we know our truths, fear of the truth revealed is viable.

Classmate
Richard Weaver

My senior year of college required me to audit and define the problems of a small business in the community. After we identified a problem or problems, we wrote a business plan, to be presented to the owner and our class.

The business I was assigned to help, a small distribution warehouse, needed an inventory control system designed to control and locate the items within the warehouse. Their main products were items imported from Germany and a few other European countries.

The warehouse inventory items were stacked on shelves with no indication of items on the shelf. The owner of the business assigned a young man to help me locate stored items and their location in the warehouse. Then we would identify the items on shelves, their point of origin, and the cost of the item.

I was given a voluminous stack of import records, over three hundred pages, and indication where the items were stored.

My first task was to design a system that would identify the items and their location in the warehouse.

The person assigned to help me was 19 years old and his job in the warehouse was his first fulltime job.

He astounded me! When I asked for location of an item, he could tell me where the item was located in the 10,000 square foot storage area. The warehouse stored over 30,000 items and he was able to identify the location of each item.

The warehouse did the majority of their business with German companies and the young man was able to converse with the German venders in fluent German.

I asked him if he took German in high school. He told me he had not, and in fact found school very boring, but graduated high school at the insistence of his parents.

"Where did you learn to speak German so well?" I asked.

"Oh, I leaned it myself."

The owner of the business told me the young man had been working for him for only a few months and learned to speak German and Spanish after he came to work.

While talking with the young man, it was very evident that he was extremely intelligent and his observational skills were far above the average person.

I invited him to attend the final presentation of my project to my college class. He accepted and sat quietly while several presentations were given.

When the presentations were complete, the professor asked if anyone had any questions. The young man made several comments and even some corrections to two of the other presentations.

When class was over the professor asked the young man if he was a graduate student from another college. The professor and all the students listening were astounded when the young man said he had just finished high school.

A few weeks after my presentation, I stopped by the warehouse to talk with the young man.

The owner told me he no longer worked at the warehouse. He moved to Canada because he got a full-ride scholarship to the University of Kings College.

High School Fight Club
Richard Weaver

Josh and Bill were seniors in high school and enjoyed the later years of a juvenile life. They were both soccer players and enjoyed the rough contact sport. Each was proud to sport an imaginary title of being one of the toughest kids in school.

When they could get some beer, they would drink a couple and try to outdo each other in stupid activities. They tried to embellish their state of drunkenness if they were at a gathering of their high school classmates.

They enjoyed berating one of their fellow classmates for not being more "manly" and not wanting to be one of the tuff guys in school. The student, Mike, was not real large, but always avoided any confrontation. One of their teachers was in the same category as the student they had been rude to on several occasions.

One Friday evening, Josh and Bill were drinking a few beers and decided to attend an amateur MMA contest and even, maybe, muster the courage to get into the ring and fight an unknown opponent.

They went into the gym and lied about their age when they signed up to fight. Each of them listed their weight as 195 pounds, which was a little more than they weighed.

They were taken to a dressing room and given the boxing gloves and groin cup. Each waited in the dressing room to be called into the ring to fight.

After a twenty-minute wait, Josh was called to the ring for a match. Bill waited for ten minutes and was called to go into the ring. Bill asked why Josh's fight didn't last very long. The response was, "Knock-out."

Bill expected to see Josh standing in the ring. Instead, the student he berated several times was in the ring.

The announcer said, "And now for our champion's second match of the evening, welcome Bill. Say hello to our reigning champ, Mike. Have a great fight!"

Dear June
Richard Weaver

Dear June,

   We had an experience over the last few weeks that I must share with you.

   A few days ago, Frank walked out of the house on his way to work. When he was midway down the front steps, a young girl walked out from under the steps and began walking toward the street.

   The girl was ten years old, dressed in pants, a long-sleeved shirt, and a blue hoody. All of her clothes were dirty and her hair was matted and unkempt. Most alarming was the state of her shoes: they were tattered and the sole of one was held on by duct tape.

   She stopped and turned to face Frank when he called to her. He asked her why she was under the porch and why she looked so cold. The girl told Frank her parents made her leave the house by five o'clock in the morning and she couldn't return until ten o'clock at night.

   Frank brought her into the house and I fixed her breakfast. May, my ten-year-old daughter, walked into the kitchen and exclaimed, "Patty, what are you doing here?" Then she began to cry.

   May explained that Patty was constantly being bullied by her classmate for the clothes she wore and her shoes at school.

   "I have tried to make friends with May, but she won't talk to me or be friends with anyone at school," Patty said.

   "I'm so ugly and so dirty, I don't want to be around anyone," May said.

   "Mom, Dad, can May take a shower? I have some clothes she can wear, and I will help her do her hair," Patty said.

   "Of course," I said. "But first, tell us why your parents make you leave the house."

   "They tell my sister and me they never wanted us and we have to stay away from them," May said.

After May showered, we put her in some of Peggy's clothes and fixed her hair. Frank drove Peggy and her to school, both with lunch money and warm coats.

I called CPS and told them of May's living conditions. CPS went to the school and interviewed May. CPS called us and asked us to house May until the courts resolved her situation.

A terrible situation!

Love,
Terry

The letter I received from June:

My Dear Friend,

I am so grateful to have such good friends who share their good fortunes with others.

We have some clothes that might fit the little girl and would be happy to drop them off.

Please let me know if there is anything I can do to help your new daughter.

Sincerely,
June

My second letter to June:

APRIL FOOLS!

The Bucket List
Pete La Combe

Now that I am 75, I have a bucket list I have been working on ever since I heard of them. Most bucket-list items were stupid—things I saw on TV and movies growing up, like entering the eye of a hurricane, chasing a tornado, riding a huge wave, even trying to be a pro surfer. Fulfilling the entries that had been on the list since my youth depended on making it back from Nam. The first thing on my first bucket list, conceived while in Nam, was to not take a dirt nap here in the bush. It all started then. I thought of all the things I would do if I made it home. As it turned out, I was one of the lucky few who did (my mortar squad had 80% casualties). Made it home, that is, with a life-changing back injury that I got after being bounced from a speeding gun-jeep. Shit happens despite your plans, so I've been told, and you must live with it. That's life; I know I got off easy.

I found myself in Harbor Jr. College, spinning my wheels except in art and gunner-mortar training. So I went for those. My experience plotting mortar rounds in Nam landed me a good job, finally, as a cartographer for the Los Angeles City Fire Department, where I drew maps, did calligraphy and made illustrations.

The next thing I knew, I had two girls. As the years flew by, they lost their baby teeth. Pulling them gave me the idea of designing a Tooth Fairy doll. Somehow, after submitting a patent search, I got two utility patents on my concept. I am finding out that there's a lot of crooks out there who will leap at the chance to feed off your dreams, like Sonos in Huntington Beach, who ripped me off. I feared I would never progress to a prototype of my doll unless I built it myself.

So I made it an item on my bucket list to do so. With the Tooth Fairy haloed in the light at the end of the hypothetical tunnel, I enrolled in MAKR 101 at Folsom College. As soon as I learn how to draw, print, and use a 3-D printer, I will design and produce a "Gold Panner Tooth Fairy Doll" to start. Believe it or not, it will bring you luck and help you find more GOLD!

It feels good to be on track again, going for it. Even if I fail, I know I gave it a shot, trying to get my idea in front of the right person, one that might want to help a Vietnam Vet, one who believes in the Tooth Fairy, perhaps? Where is Dwayne Johnson? Shark Tank?

Snake, Lizard and Rabbit Valley
Pete La Combe

I remember looking out my dad's '56 green Chevy step-side pickup, talking my dad's ear off. 'What's that? What's this? Why this? Why that?' He told me many times he didn't need a radio when I was with him, and that's why he didn't have one: just a steel plate was there. "You're the radio. Don't stop talking: you can talk the ears off a wooden Indian, son," he said more than once, laughing. He was always pulling my leg. I saw a lot of Angelenos driving around doing service calls and buying parts he needed. He owned "La Combe's Refrigeration" in Carson. Looking out the window I saw, not far from my house, people along the Main Street, fishing for crawdads—the same street that goes all the way downtown if you go north from Torrance Blvd about 15, maybe 20 miles. Many fields and small hills, laced with dirt channels that fed the flood plains, filled the Tooley-packed swampy shores. Each winter, they were full of life that stretched for miles. Little pockets of natural places became places of adventures lasting my whole childhood. One of these was beyond the end of the sidewalks, where water flowed on dirt, not concrete. I saw that nothing grows or lives on the concrete canals except the green moss that was slowly spreading toward my last refuge, a seasonal flood plain packed full of new things. A few of my friends made rafts out of repurposed junk which we floated down the middle of a 50-foot, dirt-walled canal leading to the sea. Nobody believed me back then that I saw a six-foot-long sea otter on that raft. So alarmed was it when it spotted me that it dove, leaving its half-eaten carp behind. Nobody believed me then or believes me now, but ask me if I give a shit. Once this was paradise. Here, upstream and down, was full of vegetation: life all the way, indigenous plants and animals of all kinds. Soon, though, the creeping cement finally closed in and buried it.

Writing about it now reminds me how angry I was then, and still am now, when I drive by and see nothing's left except tiny little patches, small ponds where once there was so much more. It brings a tear to my eye. Now you see these eyesores: concrete vertical walls filled with rusty shopping baskets, tires, stolen bikes tagged with paint from the local gangs (like La Rana, Keystone, Wilmas, bloods, crips, and others—all fighting like rainbow concrete or asphalt apes with guns). That a generation of cowards killed the innocence of the streets of LA is one of many reasons I am here in Placerville. I could write a whole book on the reasons.

All the last open spaces where I grew up were replaced by the San Diego Fwy, which blocked off the north side of my small world. We called it 'Snake Valley' as kids. When the Harbor Fwy was built, it ran five houses short of mine. During the planning phase, we were told we were safe being on the east side of Figueroa St. 525 west 214th Street, where I lived, was no longer a through street; now it only passed over the Harbor Fwy. My friend down the street and many more had to move. It just missed Harbor Park a mile south, which we called Lizard Valley. Farther south about a mile, on the west side, was Rabbit Valley (so-called only because we smoked out a giant cottontail rabbit into a gunny sack). Thumper (that was the rabbit's name) had it made in a 20x50 foot space, all to himself, where I kept him as a pet for many years. He enjoyed hundreds of half-cottontail bunnies after Sherry Thorn gave me a giant grey rabbit.

I hope that someday the city-planners get there their heads out of their asses and start to respect Mother Earth, who's been here long before us, and everything on it, including the natural water corridors. Build around them your modern monuments to progress that'll probably crumble into a heap or become obsolete in a hundred years! We can't forget the thousands of years it took to make these quiet special places of the past. We should spend the same amount of money and time undoing the damage mankind has done. That's what I think progress means, now that I am in my mid '70s.

37

A Place from My Childhood
William Blaylock

In the town of Vandalia, Fayette County, Illinois, west of and adjoining the Kaskaskia River, sat a large home resting on a hill. There were four or five steps leading to the porch, which stretched the full width of the home. Two wooden rocking chairs adorned the porch, a simple wooden table separating them—no banister protected the edge of the porch. A seldom-traveled two-lane Rural Route Road ran in front of the home. I heard that many years later it became a service road for Highway 40, which led to, at that time, the still unplanned Illinois State Highway 70.

One chilly, rainy night—I must have been about 5 years old—I was standing on the porch watching my grandfather walk up the hill from his car. My parents were still down at our car unpacking things to bring in from the trunk. Grandpa was wearing a heavy raincoat that covered everything but his shoes. He said, "I'll wrap you up in my coat and we can go inside and surprise your grandma and everyone." When we got inside, he said, "I have a surprise. Guess what I have under my coat?" Then he opened his coat and let me down. Grandma came running from the kitchen calling out, "Billy-John, Billy John." She stooped and hugged me. "Give grandma a kiss!" In Illinois, or in the south, or perhaps just in my family, it seemed to me that everyone was called by their first and middle names or only their initials.

Once I was able to look around the room, I saw a couch covered in red and white fabric and three plush-looking chairs. Examining my memory, I seem to remember that fabric or some kind of knitted blanket, or shawl, covered the furniture. My uncle and two aunts, who were only five to ten years older than me, looked comfortable sitting in them. The experience was fun, and I was well-received!

The house was a large home. Entering the front door positioned me in the living room. A bedroom was on the left side, and a big black potbelly stove stood near the left wall just past the bedroom door. On the other side of the stove was another door to a bedroom. Past that, leaving the living room, was the kitchen. Painted

38

light yellow, the kitchen had a round table with six chairs. Beyond the kitchen and still on the left is another bedroom (Grandma and Grandpa's). A door to the kitchen's back wall led outside to a water well and hand pump. About 30 feet beyond that was the outhouse.

A caged chicken coop was close by. A big brown barn stood atop a nearby hill. Three cows needed to be fed and milked twice daily. My uncle Tom tried to get me to milk one of the cows, but I wasn't about to stick my hands underneath that big brown-and-white animal. The next day, grandpa was sitting in the kitchen with a wooden bucket between his legs. It had a post sticking out the top and grandpa was pushing it up and down in a melodic rhythm. I asked what he was doing. "Churning butter and cream," was his reply. That evening at dinner, I got to taste Grandfather's fresh cream butter, spread on the biscuits Grandma had made on the wood-burning stove. MMM! It tasted delicious.

Speaking of Grandma and the stove—that was a mystery to me. Near the stove was a box containing split wood logs that fit just right into the top of the big black iron stove. It must have had something separating it from the stove to help prevent the firewood from spontaneous combustion. Grandma used a handle to lift a cover, then she'd toss in one or two logs, depending on how hot she needed it. Next she'd put her skillet or pot on the stove, and soon there was a hot meal. I don't know how she did it, but I thought everything she made tasted great.

"Billy-John, give Granma a kiss!"

Childhood Tales
William Blaylock

As a child, I remember watching my parents drink coffee. They always drank coffee. They had it at meals, during the day when taking a break, no matter what the time of day. In the middle of a hot, humid Mississippi day, in the evening after dinner, and when visiting with friends, they always had a cup of coffee nearby.

We tell children many tales and fables. They are told to elicit an emotion or feeling of joy, excitement, fear, bewilderment, courage, or serenity. The likes of Jack and the Beanstalk, The Pied Piper, and The Three Little Pigs, fairytales of castles, dragons, princes and princesses. Tales of meek versus bold, evil against good, ugly and wretched versus pleasant and beautiful.

I believe telling children these stories is a good thing. First, it provides them entertainment, but it also allows and encourages them to imagine and dream, creating excitement and joy for themselves. I also believe parents may choose not to tell their children these tales of wit. Truth is an excellent foundation. Sure, I remember the disappointment of finding out that Santa Claus was not real. I wanted my parents to pretend that he still existed the following Christmas. I enjoyed waking up to find a dime or quarter under my pillow, but that was easier to take than NO SANTA CLAUS!

When my wife and I were expecting our first child, I mentioned the possibility of not introducing our kids to falsehoods, like Santa and such; it's a hoax and will be a disappointment for them. I cracked. We continued the tradition because it would be more fun for the grandparents. Reflecting on that, it may allow children a gentle way to learn, and experience disappointment, and loss of a loved one; finding out that not everything in life is real. Most often, disappointments in life come from someone close to us. A parent telling their child the truth will help diminish the pain, allowing them to learn about reality. We must learn and understand this to survive the many challenges ahead, and getting a head start as a child should prove to be an advantage.

I know, I got off subject with my rant about fairytales and the like... Uh, let me see, where was I? Oh, one more thing. Are fairytales good, or are they disruptive? What is their intention? I don't want to get into that right now. I'd rather tell you a story, but as you have read, I did get into it. In fact, I became philosophical. Sorry 'bout that!

Oh yeah, back to where I started: Coffee! One day, I asked my parents if I could taste their coffee. They said I could, but that it would make the bottoms of my feet turn black. WHAT? I don't remember my response. I should have asked to see the bottoms of their feet. It would have been the proper comeback. They put a small amount of coffee in a cup, added milk and sugar, stirred it up, blew on it until cool, then let me drink. I didn't ask for more, but they told me that after drinking it I promptly inspected my feet.

In retrospect, what they should have told me was that smoking would turn the inside of my lungs black. That would have been true, although at the time they had no way of knowing what was taking place in their lungs and later mine. Thank goodness for medical science and my ability to quit smoking. I wonder what other stories they tell me, affecting my life.

I'm sure that of the many tales and fibs I've laid upon my kids, I never used that one. I shared the story with them but never tried to convince them of its truth.

Literary Therapy
Pat McCann

Therapized thoughts, oh so deep,
A provocateur, your mind will keep,
Objectively observe and put in contextual place,
Reality's occurrences should be recorded with a touch of grace.

Suffering reminds us life's in motion,
No time to rest, quell its commotion.
When the storms of life come, find an inner anchor to stay,
Otherwise, "you" could be washed away.

Be grateful for pauses, in the midst of pain,
It's a reminder to live life again.

Analyze the threat, gauge response right,
Between actual versus perceived gain insight,
Your thoughts can self-deceive,
So challenge your views, to fully achieve.

Question what you "know", for a greater truth,
Values, and positivity, are they a part of your booth?
Will they echo into the future with might,
Or fade away, like a forgotten sight?

There are no monsters in my face to fight, so the battle still lies
within
Invalidating ourselves, where do we begin?
Give what you want to get, will help the meaning revive,
Therapized thoughts on paper prove the journey and that I am alive.

Is the electrical charge in your brain,
Due to memories, driving you insane?
Perception, evidence-based so real,
The whole of you still awaits for you to heal.

Freedom and Hope
Tim Whalen

Freedom and Hope are terms that can have many meanings to many people. As I've learned in life, what one person believes to be a reward, others might see as a burden. A common example taken from my Navy Days is what's known as Liberty. For civilians, I think that would translate to the time between getting off work at the end of a work day and reporting to work the next day. They typically have an agreement with their employer to Start and Stop work at a given agreed-upon time each work-week day, and with dedicated holidays and weekends off work. The difference between that and the military is that in the military, perhaps with the exception of the (Ch)Air Force, Service Members need Leadership's permission to "have liberty" every day, because, while being in the military offers opportunities of personal freedom, you have allowed yourself to become Government Property by virtue of your enlistment, to be at the beckon call of your chain of command 24 hours a day, seven days a week, all year, every year!

In Boot Camp, it feels very similar to what I can only imagine your first day in prison feels like! You are told when and where to wake up, $#!t, pi$$, shower, shave, shampoo, eat, read, write, fold, march, stand at attention, run, walk, wait, and go to sleep! There's (at least at that time) no freedom to come and go as you please, get up "whenever," eat whatever you please, or anything like it had been on the "other side" of the fence!

Upon graduation from Boot Camp, I was assigned to attend the "A" school of my designation, which became slightly less restrictive to my freedom. While still housed in barracks-style lodging, it was up to me to get up and make it to class on time in the right clean and pressed uniform with shoes, buckles, and brass shined, hungry or full, depending on whether I chose to go get breakfast from the base galley, which for me was about a mile (seemed like 10) from the barracks, but an additional half mile back the other direction to the schoolhouse! So there were days that the rumbling of the stomach just had to wait until lunch to be satiated! Freedom here also came with a price. A young person who is free

43

from the threat of parental consequences finds himself with the freedom to screw up in a big way! The corruption of those on the other side of the gate who will happily entice you into the nefarious temptations of booze, drugs, prostitution, used car sales, and all else that is intended to make your money theirs is around every corner once you escape the cocoon of the military base. All that, and you never lose the adult responsibility of doing homework and staying focused on the highest quality of technical education that the military has to offer, and still make it back to your prison-esque accommodations in the barracks so you can get back to class early next morning!

Now that you've conquered the challenges required to pass the second phase of your military experience, you get to report to your first ship (or command, or whatever the Army does!!!). First the freedom to find my own way onto the insanely large Naval Station (San Diego), with up to 13 piers, filled with at least 50 ships that look exactly the same in their haze-grey camouflage, in an area larger than the county that I came from, carrying a fully stuffed green sea-bag and a neatly folded garment bag in which all worldly possessions are packed, looking for the ship that will take you anywhere in the world, and there she is… NOT!!! Good Old USS Downes, FF 1070, is nowhere to be found! So now you're wondering just how stupid the Navy has made me!?!?

I was afforded the opportunity to visit with the base OOD (Officer of the Day), where a few seasoned sailors stood the watch with their binders of treasured information, including the one that listed my ship as DEPLOYED on West-Pac, which, translated, means that my ship was somewhere in the far western Indian Ocean and Gulf of Oman!!! How it was decided, I don't know, but I found myself with the freedom of staying in yet another bootcamp style "open bay" barracks of their "1/2" star rated TPU (Transient Personnel Unit) where I was ordered to "check in" with the front desk every day, awaiting instructions for travel arrangements. Now WTF am I supposed to do??? Directly adjacent to the TPU barracks was the Base Theater and the Base EM (Enlisted Man's) club, complete with cheap beer that I wasn't allowed to have and the music with the disco ball that I didn't like! Great, Now What?!?

This presented me with the opportunity and freedom to explore the bus and trolly systems of beautiful sunny San Diego. I had met a few fellow "transients" in the days and evenings of hanging out at the TPU barracks, and some of us decided to go "out in town" to see this great new world. The trip to the beach(es) took a couple hours after several transfers and stopping to look around every once in a while. It was easy to see that we were completely out of place based on our childlike mannerisms, bad military haircuts, and horrendous midwestern clothing fashions!! But none of that mattered, because once we battled our way through the busy main intersection bus stop, through all the beach and tourist themed gift shops, restaurants, and bars, and the old wooden roller coaster ride, BAM! There She Blows... The wonderful splendor, in all of its expansive beauty, an ocean of ultra-hot and sun-bronzed beach babes, the most to ever gather in one place! We were in awe of the spectacle bestowed upon our eyes! This was the pot of gold at the end of any young man's rainbow of wishes! (Of course, it was look-but-don't-touch!)

So now it was time to find the real party... Tijuana, Mexico!!! Why on Earth would it be so easy for a bunch of underaged wildboys to get access to the world of debauchery and madness that is the Tijuana-USA border!?!? Once you get off the trolly, you cross through the walking gate of the border where there is zero security in place! (This was in 1985!) One of the street vendors (or was it a cab driver ?) offered a variety of items to purchase, from Chicklets chewing gum to his presumably underaged daughter!!! OMG!! Where Am I!?!? This was within the first 50 feet of entering the country, and the day was just getting started! After stopping in the first several shops, it seemed that they were all selling a version of the same crappy souvenirs. But the temptation of having an Authentic Sombrero and Poncho won me over! The price was great, but the tangible value of having "beaten" the sellers by paying them a dollar less than their asking price was heavenly... Only to later discover that you could get the same articles for less than half of what I paid! Dang It! Joke's on me!

We stopped into a few bars to beat the heat. The beer was cold and as good as I remembered it could be! On one occasion,

45

there was a bar that was doing Tequila Bombs, where you sit in a chair and lay your head back while a hottie hostess pours tequila from one bottle and mix from another bottle directly into your mouth and down your throat while counting in Spanish, Ono, Dos, Tres, Quatro... Gulp Gulp Gulp, as long as you could stand it, and then she immediately covers your mouth with one hand and shakes the back of your head with the other in order to SHAKE the drink together!!! Talk about Freedom!!! Wow!

Multiply this kind of daily activity by two weeks, and you soon realize that having this kind of freedom isn't all it's cracked up to be! I was having so much fun that I had to raise the white flag and surrender to the gods of wisdom! Some fun can be too much fun!

Eventually my orders came in, and they instructed me to get on a certain airplane at a certain time, enroute to Who Knows Where and getting there Who Knows When...

To some of our surprise, a few of the fellas that were in our little entourage ended up on the same flight. As this was official travel, and because we were stupid idiots, we boarded the plane wearing full Dress Winter Blues, or Cracker Jacks. I guess that wasn't so bad, because for some glorious reason, this happened to be a Champaign flight from San Diego to Seattle (or was it to Anchorage, AK?). Either way, it was a party for the first half of the flight, and a mass NAP for the remainder! From Anchorage, we got on a different aircraft, a C-5 Galaxy, the biggest M-Fing thing with wings I had ever seen!!! We were escorted inside the main "bay" at the rear of the plane, then up a thousand stairs to a little tiny "passenger" room, with the capacity of maybe 50 people in commercial airplane-style seats that, for whatever weird reason, faced backwards. There were no windows that I recall, and about 10 minutes into the flight they started pumping in freezing cold air throughout the small cabin, leaving me to wonder how anything could be colder than the coldest Minnesota Winter I've ever survived?!

The C-5 landed somewhere in Japan (or so we were told) in the middle of the night, something like 3 a.m., where we were instructed to get off the plane and wait in the terminal for re-fueling or some such reason and then abruptly told to re-board to our same seats. It felt so good to Thaw Out for a while. And now, onward to our "Final" (but not so final) destination of this leg of the trip. The plane landed at Clark Air Force Base in the Phillipines, where, when they opened the outer door and we showed our face to this new nation, the extreme heat and humidity that comes with this tropical nightmare of an island seemed to knock you back into the soothing frozen tundra of the C-5 AC!!! This was the most insane temperature and humidity change I'd ever felt!! I was in for a big lesson in geography and human suffering and tolerance! OMG! WHY would anyone want to live here!?!

The group disembarked and many of us were corralled into an old school bus painted in Navy Blue (or Air Force Blue!?!) and driven to the other side of the island to Naval Station Subic Bay, PI, where we were escorted to yet another "open bay" barracks that was not fitted with AC of any kind, except for the six or eight—some working, some not—ceiling fans and 'hurricane'-style slatted windows, meant to keep the air moving and the rain out. Again, a group of us were given the FREEDOM to do as we pleased for a yet-to-be-determined period of time until the admin/transient section decided what they were going to do with us. We were given enough information to answer our questions, but not enough to help us know WTF was going on. I recall a group meeting where "Doc", the base Corpsman, gave us a lecture, video, and slide show on the dangers of STDs and all the baggage that comes with it… And passed around a literal bucket of condoms for all to take! The video and slide show of various levels and phases of numerous possible STDs SHOULD have been enough to convince every man on earth to stay away from the "ladies" of the island, but, predictably, when faced with opportunity and availability, all bets were off! If you've ever wondered what it's like to visit Olongapo City, PI, just go back to the Tijuana, Mexico story and imagine it to be 100 times crazier on the Richter Scale of insane! And now imagine a 19-year-old farm-town boy with more money than ever and all the time in the world to visit all the bars in the world!! We would be in this carnival of adult fun for another two weeks (we didn't know that until the last day), until we were finally shipped (flown) out to the wonderful world of Diego Garcia!!!!

Onboard a C-5 for the second time in my life (and hopefully, but not historically, the last), a group of sailors, soldiers, airmen, and marines were on our way to Diego Garcia, the Footprint of the Indian Ocean, square in the middle of this giant ocean that I'd never heard of or studied (to my recollection)! This foot-shaped island was split in half, with the British military on one side, and the American military on the other. Three or four small islands made up the "toes" of the foot, and the "arch" of the foot made up the landing strip/base of the island. On the outskirts was raw natural deserted island (think Gilligan's Island) and the inside was a bay (harbor) that protected ships and boats from the wide-open expanse of a wild ocean. Up towards the "big toe" of the island was the U.S. Navy Base where there were admin and MWR (Morale, Welfare, & Recreation) buildings, a swimming pool, an outdoor movie amphitheater, volleyball and basketball courts, baseball diamonds, and a variety of other enjoyable activities. There were 3 "bars" on the island, one was Officers Only, and the EM club was situated overlooking the outer edge of the island. There was a beautiful beach in the "lagoon", which was a pleasant way to swim and snorkel without the washing-machine effect of the crashing waves experienced on the outer edge.

The living accommodations were slightly better than those of the Philippine base, as these were air-conditioned trailers that hosted about 12 people each, with the restrooms/showers a short walk out back. This leg of the trip proved to be a bit between Isolation Island (think: Steve McQueen & Dustin Hoffman in Papillon) and Paradise (think: Gilligan's Island). As there was nothing productive or useful to be done by our transient gang, we killed time by playing volleyball, softball, basketball, horseshoes, and a bunch of other activities during this short vacation visit.

This seemed to pass the time, and soon we were back on a bus headed to the giant mid-ocean airstrip, back on a C-5 Galaxy, enroute to the tiny nation of Oman, just 3600 km away. Once we landed, it was amazing to see actual wild camels walking in actual sand dunes to the West, and nothing but Indian Ocean to the East. This visit would be short-lived, because it seemed like only a couple hours passed before I was directed to board a gigantic (CH 47 Sea Knight) helicopter that was bound to a ship at sea. This was my first ever helicopter ride, and it was quite uneventful... Until we found ourselves hovering over the bow of a supply ship sailing at speed (about 10 knots, as I estimate). We were instructed on the next part, which was to put a horse collar device around our chest with arms out, and lifted off the floor of the chopper and lowered down the center opening in the floorboards to the ship that was not less than 50 feet below!! It was amazing to look straight up at the large egg-beater helo-blades and back inside the helo with the load master providing directions to the pilot and ship as to my "status" in flight! The few of us that were still together were escorted inside the ship and shown our quarters, the galley, and the ship's store. We each had been assigned to a 10' X 10' "stateroom" with its own bathroom/shower. Wow, I thought, this ain't so bad! It was like a hotel room and I was very impressed at the accommodations offered by Naval Ship life! Well, I would learn just a few days later, that this is NOT how "regular" navy personnel live!

A few days later, the ship (USS Kiska, I believe) pulled alongside the USS Downes FF1070, my first ship. This frigate was about 1/3 of the size of the supply ship, a lot shorter and a lot thinner. I was witnessing my first actual view of an UnRep, or Underway Replenishment. On this particular adventure, the six of us that were destined for this Fast Frigate were called to the upper deck, where cables, ropes, and pulleys were stretched from ship to ship, somehow staying above the waterline, even though the two ships, side by side, were swaying in and out, up and down, and all around. There were dozens of men on both ships holding these cables and ropes, but it wasn't until I was the last (and smallest) sailor that I took the man-lift chair-trip across the alley of ocean between the ships to land aboard USS Downes... My First Ship! Little did I know that there were actual PEOPLE holding the main cable keeping the line taut as the ships swayed back and forth. Meanwhile, another crew of people were tasked with pulling the chair/basket (think: John Wayne in the movie Midway) from one ship to the other, all while traveling forward at about 10–15 knots in good, but not completely smooth, seas! I was shocked to know THAT was how it was done, and felt relieved after I was escorted inside the skin of the ship and taken to the ship's office where I would check in, give them my military service and health records, get my berthing (living quarters) assignment, and be shown where the galley and chow hall (Dining Room for Air Force readers!) were. After I dumped my seabag and garment bag on the "coffin rack" (bunk bed with clothes storage underneath) I was given a tour of the ship and shown where my torpedo room and sonar control were. I would come to know the men and the ship very well, as this was the first day of my 4 + years aboard FF1070. This is when I learned that FREEDOM is not FREE! Being at sea, even in an All-Volunteer Military, suspends a lot of personal freedom that other Americans may never know.

Life-Changing Events in My Life
Richard Weaver

#1

As a child, I was always outside climbing trees, hiking mountains, chasing horses, or shooting birds with my BB gun. I never took time to analyze an activity, I just rushed to a completion or conclusion. I always sought to be the fastest runner, best rifle shot, and smartest kid in any class.

My preteen years were spotted with events that shaped the psyche for the trudge through my teen years. At age six I suffered a ruptured appendix and was over a hundred miles from the nearest hospital. I was near death when we arrived at the hospital and spent over three weeks in recovery.

I wasn't allowed to get out of bed for two weeks and could only stand long enough to have the bed linen changed. My parents bought me a puzzle of the United States and that was the only entertainment I had for the first two weeks of my hospital stay. I learned the location of all the states (at that time) in the United States. That knowledge stayed with me and I still remember the location of each state and adjoining states. In addition, I learned patience in completing tasks.

An adjunct lesson was in my junior year of high school. I made the football and basketball teams in my sophomore year. I felt sure I was going to be selected to play college ball and felt I was a shoo-in for either sport.

In my junior year, I was cut from the basketball team, not realizing the person who beat me worked much harder than I did in the tryouts. Later in life, I was able to see the need for work and not talk.

#2

My two weeks at Fort Bragg, North Carolina instilled the need to dig deep into yourself and find the energy and desire to achieve things you didn't think were possible. Jump School instilled in me the confidence that if there was something I wanted to do, I could do it.

I suggest the most life-changing moment came to me while working in the county jail as a deputy sheriff.

When a drunken person was arrested and put into jail, we were required to hold them for four hours or until they appeared to be sober enough to care for their safety or the safety of others.

I was assigned to work in the jail for sixteen months. During that time, I encountered some of the same people coming into and out of the jail. One of our regulars was a very pleasant person and articulate when he was sober.

On one occasion I booked our regular into jail and was escorting him to the drunk tank. For reasons unknown to him or me, he turned and struck me in the face with a closed fist.

He was easily subdued and I threw him into the cell. My anger made me wait to see if he was willing to continue the fight.

As I looked at the man the thought struck me: "That is a human being created by God and has nothing in his life that makes his life worth living. What a waste of a life. What is the common denominator for all the drunks in the tank?"

The thought was on my mind for several weeks and as I "peeled the onion", I determined the root of the drunken lifestyle was not intoxicants but a self-worth issue. I surmised the only difference between me and the drunks was that I had a belief in myself but was void of the guiding power.

I was attending a Catholic College and was required to take a religion class as part of the curriculum. I soon discovered the guide in my life had to be a greater power than I could create or that could be known to me. The class opened my mind and heart to follow the teachings of Jesus Christ. I have been striving to follow His teaching and found a life path much easier to follow than the one of others.

Thoughts of Family
Richard Weaver

Joe was sharing the foxhole with me a few hours ago. We were sharing the same freezing cold weather, the no hot meals, and the same fear of not seeing another sunrise. We often talked about our families and home. He was from Kansas and I from California.

About two hours ago, Joe walked into the surrounding trees to relieve himself when I heard the buzz of a German 88 anti-aircraft gun shell streaking overhead. The shell exploded in the trees, hitting Joe. There was nothing left of Joe! All of his gear and personal items were still in our foxhole.

Our foxhole is 100 miles west of Berlin in the middle of a war zone. The German army is in full retreat but still killing my fellow soldiers. It is starting to snow so I will use Joe's poncho to cover the foxhole and maybe I can keep some of the snow from getting in. I can't start a fire because the smoke and light from the fire will give away my position.

The German artillerymen are very accurate and the 88 is their favorite weapon to use against us.

Why am I here? It's 17 degrees, starting to snow and I haven't had a hot meal in two weeks. My feet are freezing, I have used my last pair of dry socks, and my wet pants are frozen. I will collect Joe's things and wait for the removal officer to come.

The warm California sun and my family gathering for a Christmas celebration are the only thoughts I have of the sane world I left behind.

Mom, Dad, and my sister and brother gathered around the Christmas tree laughing and sharing a large, hot meal, mom's apple pie and my sister's chocolate cake for dessert.

Two years ago, after graduating from high school, I was working at a "Go Nowhere" job and thinking of enlisting in one of the armed forces to fight for our freedom. Several of my classmates had been drafted and were off to some military training camp. I wonder if their thoughts are of family and home while living in some foreign country and trying to stay alive.

I have to find some mental relief from my situation!

I see some movement across the small opening in the grove of trees as I hold the scattered remains of Joe. Definitely a German soldier! He is stopping. I can see him reaching in his uniform and pulling out his wallet. I am looking at him now though my binoculars and see him looking at a picture.

I shouldered my M-1 and took carful aim. My bullet struck the German in the center of his chest, killing him instantly.

I wondered if he was looking at a family picture and thinking of being home for Christmas.

Echoes of Influence
Travis Dover

You weave through the labyrinthine corridors of the hospital, the soles of your shoes squeaking against the sterile linoleum floor. A cacophony of beeping machines and muffled pages over the intercom are the steady beats of the day. The weight of your white coat feels heavier today, pockets brimming with the tools of your trade.

The vibrating pulse in your pocket cuts through the din, pulling you out of the rhythm of your rounds. You glance at the screen. A text from a phone number you do not recognize.

"Hi. This is Hannah, Tod Brewer's sister. I hope you remember Tod. He idolized you in high school drama class. Got something important to share in person if possible. I'm in Folsom on work," her message reads, concise yet laden with a gravity that tugs at your focus.

You quickly compose a response without losing your stride. "Hi there. Sure. Can we meet at Reilly Park? I'll bring my wife and kids if that's fine. 4pm?"

The affirmative response arrives before you slip the phone back into your pocket. You press on, mentally juggling patient charts with this unexpected detour in your day.

As you immerse yourself in the relentless needs of your patients, the hours swiftly pass by. Then, with practiced efficiency, you shed the persona of doctor and don the role of family man. Your wife greets you at home, a hurricane of hugs and stories from five exuberant children swirling around her as you enter the house from the garage. You share the message with her and ask if it's fine they meet Hannah at the park at four.

"Sure. We can bring our dinner with us," she agrees. "Kids, get your shoes on, we're going to the park." A feeling of contentment and affection swells within you, grateful that Charlotte has enough faith in you to agree to an encounter with a woman from your past whom she was previously unaware of.

The kids excitedly fly over each other to retrieve their shoes and toys. The older kids help Mom to pile food into plasticware. You observe your eldest son sliding his feet into a matching set of sable Keene footwear, nearly identical in dimensions to the ones adorning your own feet.

At the park, leaves rustle a whispered symphony above as you all converge by an ancient oak tree. Hannah stands there waving you over, her two kids flanking her like small sentinels.

"Thanks for coming," she starts, her eyes scanning each face before settling on yours.

The kids scatter, absorbed in their games, laughter punctuating the evening air as if to underline the seriousness that hovers between you and Hannah.

"This is my wife," you utter, and Charlotte reaches out to grasp Hannah's available hand in a cordial handshake. You introduce Hannah as the sister of Tod, likely the funniest kid you encountered during your high school years.

"And he's why I wanted to meet you in person," says Hannah. "Can we have a seat on the bench?"

You and Charlotte take a seat together on the bench beside Hannah. She stares out at the children, her two mingling and running along your five.

"Tod loved drama," she begins. You notice she uses the past-tense. "He would talk about you as his inspiration all throughout high school."

Charlotte looks at you. "You don't talk a lot about your acting," she says.

"We got married and had kids," you say. "I couldn't dream anymore, I had to pay bills." You share a smile, though it is difficult given the situation.

"He talked a lot about Poe you both put on together. You were Edgar Allen, and he was your protagonist in the stories you told. That was the last play you and he performed in together," Hannah continues. "You graduated school and moved on with your life. The school wasn't the same without you. I was a sophomore when you graduated. Tod was a junior. His senior year, he took over your role. He was the lead in all the performances. He even sang! That's something you would never do," she giggles slightly.

56

"After he graduated, he went to Hollywood to do standup comedy. He was very ambitious. Unfortunately, his natural talent for quick-thinking humor wasn't what it took for standup timing and reading of the crowd. He was booed off the stage twice. The first time he thought was a fluke, that maybe that's what happened to new comedians. The second time it happened changed him. He thought maybe he should pursue acting instead. He applied for school but couldn't get in."

The children run past, and you warn the younger ones to slow down before they fall on the concrete. They are too preoccupied with their game to hear you.

"He decided to come home for some respite. Our dad wanted to get him hired on at the police department. Could you imagine Tod being a sheriff's deputy?" she laughs at the thought. "I was in and out going to school and working. He wasn't himself at all. I wish I would have consoled him somehow. But life goes on and you roll with the punches, right? But I didn't know some people didn't know how to roll. Anyway, the last time we saw Tod alive was the evening of his birthday." Teardrops well up in Hannah's eyes, and a single one trickles down her cheek, landing on her blouse.

"I'm sorry," you whisper, waiting to hear more.

You watch as she inhales deeply and then exhales, the breath leaving her lungs in a heavy sigh. "It took the police two days to find his body, and my dad's missing state-issued firearm. He did it in a field next to our house. No note. He was sober when he did it. This happened years ago, and I still can't make sense of it."

You turn toward Charlotte as she wipes at her moist eyes.

"I'm so sorry," you say.

"I've accepted it," Hannah says. "To the best I can, at least. I just wanted you to know. He so looked up to you. I felt you would probably want to know."

You don't know what to say. You peer out over the park and watch as your kids play a form of soccer on the field with a ball they had found. Your eldest son kicks it hard, narrowly missing your daughter's head. He parts his hair just like yours. He tucks his shirt into his pants the same way you do. He sees you staring at him and waves a hand that says, 'everyone's fine'.

57

You observe a gloomy, charcoal-hued cloud hanging low in the heavens. An immense pressure weighs upon your chest. The force of gravity intensifies, exerting an overwhelming downward tug. You fumble for the right thing to say, but all that surfaces in your thoughts is, "I didn't know he looked up to me so much."

Crossing Paths
Pete La Combe

It started out like every other normal workday: dragging my head off the pillow at 4:30 am, walking (or running, if I was running late) west down Dodsworth toward the RTD bus stop and catching the five o'clock Express Bus 422, from Covina to Downtown Los Angeles. If I had a good book to read, the time flew by. We were the last stop leaving (Temple and 1st Street) but the first stop returning, when it was easy to get a good seat. It was a short walk west down Main Street to City Hall East, 200 North Main Street, and up to the 10th floor to the Maps Drafting Unit, Los Angeles City Fire Department. I was a cartographer, graphic designer, and calligrapher for 20 years. I always took my job serious, trying my best to provide for the guys on the ground—the 'Grunts', the Paramedic drivers and Firemen—with the most accurate maps possible. I hoped I had a small part in bringing down the response time and saving a person's life. From my experience in Vietnam as a mortarman in Delta Troop 1/9 Cavalry, I knew that time is your enemy, here as much as there.

The only thing I remember about this day at work was that, for some reason, I didn't catch the bus at the first stop; I can't even remember why I walked through old city hall and down the steps to Spring Street. I caught the bus on the second stop (Temple Street and Spring); I was there waiting with at least 20 people. In line a few people back from the northeast curb, I saw the light turn green, then a rush of people started coming east toward us, a few stragglers left behind. Just as the light changed from yellow to red, I noticed the last cross-walker was box-stepping, drunk as a skunk. Everybody was watching; he was so drunk nobody could believe it. When finally he tried to step up on the curb, he fell flat on his back in the street, not noticing the curb was taller than usual because he was so fucked up. He even kept walking as if he was still on his feet.

It all happened in a spit second: an RTD bus driver, seeing the light green, punched the gas pedal to make the hill, not seeing the man lying in the crosswalk. While everybody stood there in a frozen shock, I pushed through the crowd, reaching down to pull him to his feet and onto the sidewalk a second before the bus shot past us.

59

Unaware of what had just happened, the drunk walked off toward the homeless camps along the 101 freeway. He didn't say or notice anything, but we all saw him pull out a broken pint-bottle of vodka from his right back pocket which washed down and off his leg onto the street as he walked away. Now and then, I look back on that day and wonder why we made that connection at that moment in time, and hope he remembered just how close he came to being crushed that evening by that RTD bus. I know for a fact that everyone there on that corner that night knew I changed that man's life, and saw he was so drunk he didn't even know I saved it.

Norman
Pete La Combe

When I was a kid (I mean under 10), my world grew when I learned to walk to school the long way. I walked east on 214th street, taking a right on Moneta Avenue. I crossed Carson Street and went into my favorite liquor store, "Sandy's Liquor". It wasn't the way I was told to walk to school, but I liked going this way because Norm, about the only grown-up who was always ready to tell and hear good stories, worked there. When he was younger, he grew up in Hawaii. I thought of him as a wise man. Being so young, I knew I had a long wait before anybody thought me to be wise, if ever. He had a way of telling stories such that I could almost see them as I listened. He told me once, "Back in WWII, when I was a young man, Navy sailors, when they were on leave, would disembark and, seeing me minding my own business, try to teach me a lesson for being Japanese."

I was confused. I asked, "What kind of lesson?"

"Some people must be taught a lesson. I taught many Navy Guys—some black, some brown, some white—that I'm just as American as any of them. Telling me, 'go back to Japan, Gook,' I retorted, 'my family's been here in Hawaii many generations: you assholes just got off the boat.' I had fun in my younger days teaching sailors, 'don't mess with the little guy.' Just because you're at war with Japan doesn't mean you're at war with me or can kick my ass back to Japan. This is my home. I am just as American as you are. I didn't tell them I was a fourth-degree black belt before I kicked their butts six-at-a-time once. I told them, 'And I'll kick your ass again, you round-eyed punks! We all have foreign ancestry! I'm just as American as you!'"

He always made me laugh (he called me 'round-eye' whenever I came in).

I knew at an early age I was one-third American Indian from both sides of my family. Norm's lessons taught me that we all belong here, except the assholes.

Monty De Parted
Pat McCann

Monty was a man who built a fortress of solitude around him to protect himself from life's trials and tribulations. However, this isolation left him yearning for connection and companionship.
One day, his eyes were trapped by a vision with curves and soft skin that captivated and crippled his defensive guard.
He watched from the ramparts as she strolled in the front gate unchallenged.
No alerts, alarms, or calls to arms were given or heard.
He met her on a downhill slope that became an uphill battle.
Looks that were meant to kill now drew first blood.
Even so, his perception of her goodness left him disarmed.
Now armless, her darker intent reveals itself.
Now lured by attraction and lamed by his lust.
Now he notices that he no longer has legs to stand on,
Excuses don't bother covering for the judgment lapse.
With no flipping appendage, he lies on the ground with eyes pointing upward.
Pointlessly searching for why, a thought occurs.
Before he loses it, his head shakes much to his dismay,
It moves this way until all attachment is lost.
This should be the end, but more insults are to come.
They say love is blind as his latest flame set him ablaze.
Being killed with cliche his last thoughts smolder,
She didn't care enough to even piss on me when I was on fire.
Walking off with consciousness clear, but how you say,
She is so skilled at the lies that she even believes the ones she tells herself.
New realities are made when truths don't serve her story-tellin'.
For time to heal all wounds, surviving the aftermath is required.
Love doesn't conquer all;
just the ones like Monty that aren't lying when professing it.

From the bar called The Beyond, the spirit of Monty now drinking in rum spirits says to you,

"You didn't see my life book just one of its last chapters for some of the prior ones were quite good.

"Firstly, allow me, to advise you to use more discernment in whom you give the keys to the castle than I did.

"Next… Yes, the Queen of Spades put me down.

"But life is guaranteed to pour you shots of suffering and pain, suck it all up buttercup.

"Cause you might gain enough meaning and measures of pleasures to make it worth it."

Drinking one, his mug brews up another sharp tip,

"Those within hugging or striking distance, extra attention must be paid.

"When it goes wrong, do what I couldn't in the end,

"Pull yourself back together and push on.

"You take the good with the bad even when the ending is sad.

"From once a king of the castle on the hill to a head rolling down to rest, as guardian of the gutter,

"Cheers!"

You Will Do What I Say
Richard Weaver

During my law enforcement career in the San Francisco Bay Area, I worked as an Intelligence Investigator, in Undercover Narcotics, on the Executive Protection Team, and as a sniper on the SWAT Team, a Patrol Deputy, and Patrol Sergeant.

As my family grew, my wife and I decided to move the family away from the rampant illegal drug use and the general atmosphere of a large city. We eventually settled in a small rural county in South East Idaho. I was hired on a six-man police department.

A short time after I began working for the department, I was approached by some citizens who asked me to run for county sheriff. I was elected and took charge of a twelve-person department. It was a rude awakening and step back in time.

The department uniform was a light brown shirt with dark brown epaulets and dark brown pocket flaps. The badge was less than a half dollar in size, with lettering so small that reading it was near impossible.

There was no standard department weapon and each deputy carried whichever revolver caliber and size he wanted. With no standard pants or shoe regulation some deputies wore blue jeans or some shade of brown pants. No necktie or hat were used by the deputies.

The patrol vehicles were SUVs and all had rifle racks in the back window with no lock to keep the weapon safe from theft. However, several of the deputies carried fishing poles in the rack, maybe to avoid the theft of a rifle.

My first order was blue jeans were not allowed to be worn as part of the uniform. Second, I was going to get standardized police leathers for everyone and a standard weapon would be issued by the department.

While waiting for the weapons and leather to arrive my instructions were: the caliber of the weapon had to be a .38 caliber and revolvers had to be a double action.

I told the deputies that as standard procedure I would periodically inspect their weapon before they went on patrol. The day after my ultimatum on weapon readiness, two old-timers, each carrying a revolver, reported for the day shift. I had them unholster their weapons and open the cylinders. Both opened the cylinders of their weapons and I instructed them to empty the cartridges out of the weapon. Neither of them could get the ammunition out of the weapon. Each explained they had not fired their weapon for four or five years. The bullets were so corroded they had to pry them out with a pocket knife.

One of the deputies, whom I will call Walt, was carrying a single action .41 magnum in a buscadero holster and belt. The holster was slung to the middle of his thigh and tied to his leg with a leather strap.

The new weapons and leather had not arrived so I took no action to correct his weapon or his holster.

A few days later, Walt reported for work wearing a uniform shirt with a "gravy" stain on the front, blue jeans with a tear in the knee, and white tennis shoes. His weapon was at mid-thigh and there was no safety strap holding the weapon in the holster.

I became a little excited and told Walt to go home and put on some decent clothes. Further, he was not getting paid until he came back to work looking like a deputy sheriff instead of a hobo with a gun.

Walt came back to work wearing the same torn blue jeans, white tennis shoes, and his weapon at half-mast on his leg. However, he did follow my order and was now wearing his new blue western shirt with his badge proudly pinned on his chest.

To my chagrin, Walt did as I asked. He obeyed my order to the letter, in his world, and missed my intention.

65

The Elk Hunt
Richard Weaver

The Sawtooth Mountains in Western Idaho are rugged and heavily forested with Log Pole and Saratoga Pine trees. A few Forest Service Trails wandered through the mountains and often led to a small lake or another water source.

Two friends and I decided to plan an Elk hunting trip into one of the most rugged parts of the mountain range. We planned for a four-day hunting trip and packed the necessary supplies for us and our horses.

I was proud of my new 30.06 Winchester with an 8 to 12 variable Weaver Scope. The scope enabled me to hold a three-inch shot group at 300 yards.

We arrived at the trailhead parking lot in the mid-afternoon and decided to stake the horses, spend the night, and start into the mountains in the early morning. (This adventure took place before air mattresses.) Although I was warm, the ground was hard and I did not get much sleep.

The trek into the mountains was arduous for both the horses and the riders. We often had to get off the horses and lead them up the steep mountainside. Parts of the trail were loose rock and proved to be very difficult for the horses to walk on. Plus, it would have been very dangerous to try and ride a horse over that part of the trail.

We were about seven miles into the mountains and decided to make our base camp. The seven-mile trip took almost eight hours. The horses were as exhausted as we were. This was the second Elk hunt I had been on and had high hopes of taking an Elk. Of all the wild meat I have eaten, Elk is by far the most desirable.

At sunrise the next day, we went in different directions to begin our hunt. We agreed to not go more than an hour from camp and plot our compass readings every 20 minutes.

My horse was tired from the previous day's trip and was slow to react to my urgings. I eventually reached the top ridge of the mountain and got off my horse to survey the valley below. I estimated the valley floor to be about 1,000 yards from me and my horse.

I staked the horse and sat on a rock overlooking the small bowl-shaped valley and spotted an Elk grazing on the valley floor. The Elk was very large, about a 12-pointer and probably a 600-pounder. It was a trophy animal, for sure. I knew it would be necessary for me to get closer to the Elk to make a shot.

I started to lead my horse and walk down the steep sloop of the mountain and the horse balked. I knew that if I took time to attend to my horse the trophy Elk may be gone before I could kill him. I dropped the reins of the horse in hopes it was too tired to run off and walked and slipped down the mountain. When I reached a distance from the Elk where I felt I would be able to make the kill, I stopped and unshouldered my rifle.

Another look at the Elk fueled my hope of taking such a trophy. I made the shot and the Elk immediately dropped. I struggled down to the animal and made the necessary cuts to have him bleed out.

I looked up at the top of the valley wall and saw my horse still standing. I was still ablaze with the pride of taking such a large animal and again looked up the mountain. How am I going to get him out of here? The horse won't come down here—the Elk is too big to carry up. If I quarter the animal, I still can't carry that much weight.

I thought, "Good shot but poor planning." Many hours later and several trips down to the valley floor, our hunting party managed to get the Elk back to our base camp.

Last Preparations
Travis Dover

"And as it is appointed unto men once to die, but after this the judgment" - Hebrews 9:27

The old man stared down at his fingers. The edema made them flat, white, and insensitive. They weren't what he remembered. Neither were his feet. He hadn't felt them for a year. Or maybe it was ten years. The highways of nerves were damaged and beyond repair like much of his body. He stopped shaving altogether as the thing in the mirror was unfamiliar and frightening, the yellow specter staring back at him with its sunken cheeks and gaping jaw and eyes.

His hands shook uncontrollably as he counted batteries and flashlights he had brought in from the garage. He had many toys—as he called them—items he ordered to his house over the years that were almost all new, used once and forgotten. No big retirement savings, but a lot of cold steel items that either plugged in, threatening eardrums, or that spat fire, or kicked up dust. His friends and family would never describe him as handy, but he enjoyed crafting with what he had. He once had spent an entire day off from work working on the dryer, replacing the drum's belt. It could have been done cheaply and quickly by someone keen on such repair work, but he liked doing things himself. The machine made a terrible noise whenever used after that.

What was he doing now? Counting. He lost count. He slid the batteries into a cardboard box beside some tactical flashlights. A new thought occurred to him. He walked toward his bedroom, stretching a hand out once and a while to feel for a wall or table, careful not to trip over a small dog. He returned to the living room half an hour later with his walker. On its seat was an ammo can and pistol. Beside it, balanced with his free hand, was a large case that contained his carbine. He rolled it up beside his hospice bed in the living room and sat at the mattress's edge. He stared forward out the back door over his mobile armory. The sliding glass door was hazy with years of not being maintained, having needed to be replaced years ago. The carpet near it was torn up by dogs. Fur and crumbs speckled the old flattened, coffee-colored carpet.

His son watched him from the dining room table. He had seen his father's preparations for years, long before his father's first jaundice, the cancer, long before the surgeries, therapies, and now this second and last jaundice. His dad had always bragged about his solid biceps. They were metabolized now, and the bone of his arms and face protruded like something uncanny. Green veins ran over and down his forehead and face. This series of preparations his son watched started decades before when he was a just a child.

He watched his dad then rent movies and create VHS copies. Hundreds of these copies of movies still existed in a wardrobe in the first bedroom down the hall. He watched as his dad printed out piles of papers on aliens and mysteries of the world. A dozen original newspapers about Reno's flood of '97 were air-vacuum-sealed and stored in a drawer somewhere as time capsules. His dad collected ammo and guns throughout the years, enough for a local revolution. His father was always hoarding, collecting, preparing. Years-old emergency food was stored in a closet somewhere. And now, after thirty-nine years, his son registered what the business was about, and for what the preparations. His father made it known on many occasions he would put a bullet in his brain before dying of cancer like his father. Now, the bullets were there for his and his wife's protection. Protection from what?

"Fuck." The word traveled out like a rough wind from his father's mouth. He wasn't wearing his dentures. He had no appetite, so the teeth weren't necessary.

"What is it, Pa?"

"Oh," he said, then trailed off. After a moment, he turned boyishly to his son and said, "Don't get old."

"What are you doing with all the guns and ammo?" asked his son. "You look like you're going to war."

His dad looked at the weapons and ammo can. He put a shaky hand out and stroked the rifle case. "Who knows? With all those black-lives-matter anarchists, and terrorists," he mumbled another inaudible sentence, then grinned a little. Turning more toward the dining room, he said in a slightly mocking accent, "One day, son, this will all be yours." He had said the same line jokingly countless times to his son over the years, usually about his tools.

"Well, why is it out here?"

"When I die, you mom will be alone," he said. "She will need protection."

The son smiled a little. "She can hardly move herself. She'd probably trip over her oxygen lines trying to get to a gun."

The father nodded and mused, "Probably shoot herself," he said. It was a joke, but Mom had shot herself in the leg when they were younger. She wasn't now the same out-of-control drunkard who battled sins like she did when she was in her thirties. The son studied his aged mother in the recliner with her eyes closed and hearing aids out on the coffee stand beside her. Amazing how careless healthy young people can be with their lives, then so frail and helpless, yet clinging to life, in old age. Cancer would kill his dad very soon, but Mom was in for even worse suffering: end stage COPD and loneliness.

Both parents took their naps, Mom in her chair, Dad in his hospice bed. The son knew this would be the last time he saw his dad, and he knew he wasn't fully registering this information in the present and would need to revisit it later, after. When? He didn't know. He had a wife, kids, work, bills. Life would go on. Unlike the saints who prayed for unification with God before death, his dad prepared with guns and ammo and flashlights. He thought he was preparing and fighting, but he was going about it the wrong way. He always had gone about things the wrong way. He worked more when he and mom fought. He drank more beer to relax. He collected things instead of having relationships. He prepared for the end of the world with jugs of water and cases of food in his son's old bedroom. Now the end had come, and none of his things would save him.

The son packed his stuff back into his car while his parents napped. He phoned his wife to let her know he was leaving and should be home in a few hours. After the dogs barked the third and fourth time he had walked in and out the front door while packing his car, both parents had stirred awake.

"I need to get going if I'm going to beat the traffic," said the son.

His mom stood. "It was so nice that you were able to come out and visit, even if it was for just a couple days. We'll walk you out," she said.

"Oh, no, no need for that," said the son. His father was already rocking upward from a sitting position, his face in a constant pain-filled expression. The little bit of hair he still had was a mess. The cane his son purchased for him hung on the side of the walker near the rifle. Once his dad was upright, he wobbled, and began walking toward the small foyer, reaching toward walls and stable items. The son was about to tell him to use his cane, but knew it was of no use. Even after watching him fall the day before when he tried to break up a fight between his dogs, he knew his dad was resigned to risks and falls. He wouldn't use walking assistance. That was for the guns.

They were outside in the driveway. Parents hugged their son in turn. The son made little eye contact with the father and stepped into his car to leave. But then, the father gave his son one last gentle squeeze with his thumb and finger at his son's elbow. It was slight, and no one would have known anything from it, but that extra insignificant display of affection was his dad's way of saying goodbye. A hundred times before, they would have said, "Till next time," or "See ya soon," but not this time. The quiet stillness was deafening. The son gave them a wave as he backed down the driveway, his face muscles tightening, his stomach heavy and sour, and he allowed himself to cry a little as he made his way home over the hills.

What A Blast
Pete La Combe

I am not sure when I lit my first firecracker, but I was hooked ever since my dad bought me a whole block of Black Panthers while on vacation in Colorado. I never lit them except once they were all tied together, in which configuration they didn't last as long. One at a time I lit them with my magnifying glass. It was the most fun blowing plastic Army men and jeeps up in the air for hours. Never in my wildest dreams would I have believed I would be blowing things up for real less than ten years later.

But here I am, still having a blast, blowing up dud rounds that were shattered just about anywhere you could imagine. There were so many small mortar rounds and 500-pound bombs dropped from B-52 bombers over the years, so many round water-filled craters in places looking like a shot-up disco ball from the chopper rides, reflecting the changing, colorful sunsets. Flying by all of the many mirrors gave the illusion that the earth below me was rotating horizontally instead of vertically.

I volunteered to be demo man soon after getting there—C-4, det cord, and blasting caps became my new toys of war. Plastic to the real thing: was that the real plan all along? Who knows? My goal was to destroy anything that could be used against us, and maybe even save a life after this FLICKING WAR.

The demo bag had twelve pounds of C-4. It came out each day and was used up long before I ran out of dud rounds, having to leave many behind. As the months passed, I got pretty good at blowing shit up. I don't know how the phrase came to me one day, when we came out of the field back to LZ Nancy after thirty days out in the bush. I thought, *We need somebody to blow some shit up before we give LZ Nancy back to the millions of rats.* I guessed there were a thousand rats for each soldier.

I was told to report to the captain in charge of the ammo dump, who showed me a pit filled to the top with old wet bullets, artillery rounds, grenades, claymores, mortar rounds, anything explosive. They gave me 200 pounds of C-4, a roll of det cord and

72

blasting caps. They told me the pit was over 10 feet deep, and the worst part was that, short of one foot from the top, it was filled with water. The captain said to let him know when I finished setting the charges. It took till past three o'clock: six hours in the hot sun. It was the most C-4 I have ever used by far, and who knows—I sure as hell didn't—how many pounds of explosives were under water. I laced hundreds of feet of det cord from bomb tip to bomb tip. It looked like a tangled mess of white clotheslines. I did the best I could wrapping the det cord around the biggest bombs, trying to get them to blow downwards and set off the rounds under water. I checked and rechecked my work and had the captain in charge inspect the muddy bomb soup which would soon be blown sky high. He walked around, looking through his binoculars, checking if I used enough charges in the right places. He gave his OK and said he would take over the rest.

Within an hour, we heard bullhorns giving warning to move away from the blast site. This went on for an hour. I was over a quarter mile away when I got the order: "Fire in the Hole!" Countdown started at 10. Ten, nine, eight, seven, six, five, four, three two, one—I yelled fire in the hole and pushed the plunger. What I saw was the biggest blast that I ever would see. The sound wave punched me in the stomach and lifted me off the ground in a dust cloud. I watched as the dust cloud rose hundreds of feet in the air, throwing unexploded ordinance skyward in all directions, most of which rained down on the downhill slope, though some landed inside the wire. The huge blast knocked everybody's socks off, and somehow not everybody got the word of the blast. The ones that didn't get the word were knocked off their feet, thinking Charlie was ready to overrun LZ Nancy the next minute. I heard later that the captain in charge got his ass chewed out big time. Luckily nobody got hurt, just ringing ears for a couple days.

That day, when the shit hit the fan, it missed me and hit the ammo captain. Luckily for me, I was only following his orders. It was a blast for me, but not for him. Glad I'm not a lifer!

73

Unknown Hero
Richard Weaver

Early in my law enforcement career I was assigned to work a swing shift, 4-12, in a very busy, high-crime area. Many calls for service during the shift were a usual night's work for deputy sheriffs working in that area.

Our response to calls for service generally required gathering information from a victim of the crime, then writing a report of the incident. The victims were usually very emotional and demanded we immediately solve the crime (just like cops do on TV).

The minority of calls involved physical altercations between people which required law enforcement to use physical force to defuse the conflict. The resolution sometimes required wrestling with one or both of the combatants.

At the end of the shift, I was mentally and physically spent. The half-hour drive home was a mild sedative to help my body and mind recover from the exertion of the activity I encountered during my shift. However, I still needed some time to "unwind" when I got home.

My "unwind" ritual consisted of taking off my gun belt, unloading my pistol, checking the ammunition to ensure it was not corroded, changing out of my uniform, and then checking on my sleeping family.

One night I completed my "unwind" routine and could not find a suitable snack to eat. I decided to get dressed and drive to the super market several blocks from my house and buy something to eat.

I got dressed, put my off-duty pistol in my belt, and drove to the store.

After choosing my snack I found it necessary to stand in line to pay for my food. It was two o'clock in the morning. "What are all these people doing here at this time of day?" I thought. My irritation level began to rise and I soon became anxious to get back home and relax.

Standing in line behind me was a man in his late twenties. He appeared to be in good physical condition, and his facial expressions showed signs of frustration at standing in line.

A man and woman were standing in front of us in the waiting line. They were engaged in a loud, heated argument.

The man grabbed the woman by the shoulders and screamed, "You stupid, ugly bitch," and with a closed fist struck the woman in the face, knocking her to the floor.

My first impulse was to grab the attacker, but I thought, "I am not in uniform and the attacker may attack me." My second impulse was to draw my pistol from under my shirt and hold him at gun point.

"Not in uniform—showing a weapon may cause panic in other customers or lead to a violent reaction from the attacker."

My split-second decision-making process was interrupted by the young man standing behind me. He pushed me aside and hit the attacker in the side of his head with his fist.

The attacker went to the floor and was doing the "chicken dance", feet and hands twitching, his eyes rolled back in his head. The attacker was unconscious and the woman had a nose bleed.

Hoping to avert more confusion, I showed my badge and told the checker to call the police. The conscious female was still lying on the floor. I checked the attacker and found a pulse, but he was still unconscious.

Moments later, two uniformed police officers arrived and took charge. I told them of the man attacking the woman and the young man behind me knocking the attacker out.

I looked for the young man who ended the attack on the women but did not see him. The checker told me, "After the man hit the attacker, he put five dollars on the counter and walked out of the store."

I had to admire the young man who ended the fight between the man and woman. He made a decision in a split second as I was still trying to sift through my options.

Overnight Business Trip
Richard Weaver

I was parking my car at the airport parking garage preparing to go on an overnight business trip. I didn't pack a suit case for the trip. I just stuffed some clean underwear in my briefcase.

I walked to the rear of my car and noticed two men standing behind an older-model four- door Ford. They were talking in hushed tones. I didn't pay much attention to them and began walking to the garage elevator.

One of the men raised his voice and said, "This is your last chance." The elevator opened and I stepped in.

I went to the airline ticket counter to check in for the flight.

"I'm sorry sir, but you flight has been delayed for an hour," the ticket agent said.

I sat in the waiting area and began working on my business plan for tomorrow's meeting. I looked up and saw one of the men who had been standing behind the old Ford in the garage carrying two very large briefcases. The briefcases resembled the ones attorneys carried, but larger.

The man sat in a chair several seats from me, but facing me. He put the two briefcases on the chair next to him. He had a furrowed brow, and his jaw muscles were twitching. "A very nervous fellow," I thought.

"Attention please—the flight to Omaha will be delayed for another hour. We are sorry for the delay, which is due to weather conditions".

The announcement seemed to cause more anxiety for the man with the briefcases.

Eventually, the man approached me and asked, "Would you mind watching those cases for me? I need to use the bathroom, and I don't want to carry them."

"No problem," I said. "I will go move closer to them."

The man walked away, and I sat next to the brief cases.

Fifteen minutes passed, and the man hadn't returned.

Soon another announcement of another one-hour delay came over the intercom.

"Wow," I thought. "Thirty minutes, and the man and still hadn't returned. I better go check on him." I started to walk to the bathroom, then decided to put the briefcases on a luggage cart and push them to the bathroom.

I was unable to locate the man in the bathroom and began to wonder if he had met with foul play of some sort. "I have plenty of time," I thought. "I will take the briefcases back to the car. Maybe he is there having some kind of medical emergency."

Back in the garage, I could not find the old Ford.

"Now what?" I thought. "I'll open one of the cases and see if there is some identification inside of it." I opened the case and gazed upon the surprise of my life: Hundred-dollar bills in stacks, bound by paper wrapping, with "TEN THOUSAND DOLLARS" stamped on the wrapper.

I opened the second briefcase, which also held stacks of hundred-dollar bills, wrapped in a paper binding, with "TEN THOUSAND DOLLARS" on each stack.

In the second brief case was a note, which read, *This money is now yours, don't call the cops.*

"Now what?" I thought. "Dope money, organized crime money. money laundering? If I give it to lost-and-found the owner will never be located and some clerk will be very rich. Don't call the cops. This could be very dangerous or very profitable."

I sat in my car, trying to weigh the pros and cons of my dilemma, when the announcement came: "The flight to Omaha is now landing and will be boarding passengers in thirty minutes."

"Do I leave with 500,000 dollars from an unknown source OR make the meeting tomorrow?" I thought.

My text to my business associate read, "Reschedule tomorrow's meeting for next week!"

Seeking Love
Richard Weaver

The melodic strings played in a broken heart
A love long lost with tears of sorrow.
Now we live an earth apart
And know within me - no tomorrow.

The days of glory and passion young
Filled our lives with bliss so deep
On a land where love once sprung
The land long past beneath my feet

Love was found more oft than not
My heart betrothed to someone new
To search my heart for love I sought
And finding love from many and few

The morning bright will fill my soul
And I shall see the one I seek
Sleeping near me to make me whole
Then my love has reached its peak.

Thoughts of yester year still haunt my brain
But the one I love shall cleanse my thought
I will live in a world close to sane
With the strings of love for which I sought.

Girl from San Pedro
Pete La Combe

It was the summer of '68. When we met, I was hanging out in the parking lot of "The Grand". It was an old theater in oldtown Torrance that had been converted into a dance hall in the mid '60s. I never went in: I thought dancing with waves was my thing and more fun, and it didn't give me the nervous sweats. Most guys just stopped by long enough to find out if there were any parties happening and get surf report from local surf rats. Most guys hung out in the parking lot, testing their skills hitting on the chicks coming and going.

That's what I did. In fact, I never went in after the theater closed. I thought I would have better luck scoring in the parking lot, though it never even happened once (one girl told me to piss off after a few minutes, and another gave me a false number). It was a Friday night after work when I drove there in my '67 Triumph Spitfire. The night I met Diane, I was leaning on my car trying to look cool, talking shit with a few jerks from the beach and Carson High, smokin' and jokin'. A carload of babes pulled in playing "Light My Fire" by The Doors full blast, singing almost as loud. I thought to myself, *Were they playing it on purpose as they pulled up? Yeah, right. Keep dreaming fool.* I only had one pickup line back in the '60s. It's only worked on a few chicks, and that was, "Do you want to get high?" It saved a lot of time chasing around a chick that wasn't a pothead like me. The ones that told me to "FLICK OFF" didn't like me saying, "Bend over on your belly." I knew quickly they were buzzkills, no bueno babes, in my book.

I heard the girl sitting shotgun say, "I want to get high, surfer boy. My friends like dancing; I'd rather cruise to the beach with you. I can tell you're harmless."

I said, "Sure. That sounds like fun, girl." I thought she had a super pretty face (a 10), with bright, blue-green eyes that had sparkle. I'd never seen a smile that real before, in any girl. I noticed she was overweight. (I was a plump kid myself till I started surfing.) Her sweet voice and sparkle made me say, "Hop in," without thinking, and "Let's go, girl." When she got out, we all noticed she was way over 300 pounds.

One of the butthead surfers standing around said, "Beached whale. Put her back in the water."

I never liked mean people and turned around and said, "You say something, shit for brains, you pizza-faced ugly FLICK?" Then I got in his face, saying he looked like a beached turd that rolled up on the sand. Dick lived up to his name: a real "DICK".

I drove off listening to Diane's friends and others ripping him a new asshole. I found out she was a sweetheart with thick skin. She was smarter than me, with goals like going to school. I didn't know what goals were, didn't know I would have a future with Viet Nam staring me in the face, hovering in front of me like a chopper blowing a wall of dust into my eyes for two years. I never told her I was enlisted in the Army. I told her I was a beach bum with an income, working at Todd's Shipyard. Then she told me she lived just down the street from Todd's. We started hanging out over that summer (my apartment being close to Todd's, PCH and Western, she stopped by all the time).

I don't know how it started, but the ten-unit apartment manager told the people who complained about the noise past 10 pm on weekends to move, and they did. All he asked was to be cool, no fighting or causing any trouble (he was an old hippy that liked to party). We called it the plaza. (He had an old Studebaker Plaza. Did he come up with 'meet me at the Plaza?' I leave it to you to decide.)He would walk around with a big flash, making sure buzzkills go somewhere else. We even had bouncers of all disciplines of karate, judo, etc. We only told chicks about the plaza and the live music.

Bill Kelso was the best musician I ever knew: he could play the guitar, banjo, piano, harmonica, flute, and more. He won a scholarship in ceramic arts, and man that guy could play the guitar (12- or 6-string) and bass. It got quiet quick when we started playing the guitar—sometimes the one-bedroom, one-bath pad became a

80

standing room. (When he got the word, he would be there.) Man, what a time.

I never figured out how it happened that three different times I woke up butt-naked on top of her. Whenever on those occasions I would awake, she would put her clothes on, run out the room, and leave. She told me she knew since she was a kid that she was fat as hell and so couldn't stand me or anybody seeing her naked.

The last time it happened I told her, "I guess this is date rape Diane, and it ain't cool, but I am not pissed off, girl, I am actually sort of flattered, but you know if you're trying to lose weight, you can back off on the sweets by eating fruit instead, right? I was lucky I found surfing, peddling my bike 10 miles each way got me off my ass. I used to be so fat that I was picked by the coaches on track- and field-day for the fat-kid tug-of-war competition, where the fattest boys in school were picked one at a time. I was always one of the first picked; I couldn't even get my arm around my surfboard till a year later, when finally I got that damn longboard off my head. If I can do it, you can too."

She gave me a kiss and left. In September I joined the Army. Four months later I was deployed to Viet Nam. A year later, Fort Hood for my last six months of active duty. Home two years later.

It wasn't too long before I visited the plaza. Short hair felt strange back then; nobody wanted the military look in the '70s (Even the coaches I had in high school who used to have buzzcuts had long hair now. Maybe they got spit on too?) A few of my 4-F friends showed up saying, "I didn't think a dumbass like you would make it home in one piece."

Sorry to disappoint you, but I can vouch it was nothing but luck in my mortar squad that divided the casualties (80 percent of us) from the survivors. Now that I'm home for good, I'm going to catch up on my wave count by snaking all the Grimmy's waves I can find. Man, it's good to be back on the water. Who knows? Maybe the seawater will wash the rest of the red dust out of my toenails.

"Did anybody tell you that Diane, the fat chick, came by looking for you a year after you enlisted? Nobody, and I mean nobody, recognized her. Everybody jumped up and started hitting on

81

her. She told all of the people that were mean to her, 'I'm the beached whale, remember me now?' One at a time she told us to go get fucked and left, laughing and calling us losers." She was right, fool. As it turned out, we never met again.

A Selfless Man
Richard Weaver

The storms of life cast to and fro, the path a man must often go,
And bring to life joy and pain, where glee and sorrow often rain,
We seek a path to lead us where love and kindness eagerly grow.
That we may live with peace of mind and find the life where love
may flow,
Or, touch a life in a way, that all may live a gentler way.
And share with him your knowledge gained through toil, sorrow and
sometimes pain,
Help him explore an unknown skill that opened his mind and an
emptiness fill.
To teach the soul of a man unknown and help him to write his life
plan with his gift from your helping hand,
Comes now to vets a soul and man that led us to a bigger plan,
The man we call, Jack Carman.

Three Things I Was Told Not To Do
Richard Weaver

#1

We lived on a cattle ranch in Idaho, and riding horses was part of the lifestyle. We were taught how to saddle and bridle horses, how to mount and dismount from them, and how to tie the reins securely.

My father was a horse trader, and we often got a new horse to add to the herd. He would ride the new horses to make sure they were suitable for use in our work. He once traded an Arabian for a small Paint.

The Arabian was headstrong and would often just start running for no apparent reason. Even with a broken bit in his mouth, stopping him was a task no 12-year-old could do easily.

The Paint we got was easy to catch and didn't show any signs of aggression to me when I fed or petted her. My dad told me not to ride the horse until he got back from the auction of some of our cattle in Idaho Falls (about a four-hour drive from the ranch). He told us, "If the auction goes long, I will stay in Idaho Falls with my uncle for the night."

It was late afternoon, my chores were done, and there was nothing for my brothers and I to do. I suggested we saddle the Paint and ride it for a while. My brothers reminded me of the instructions Dad gave us about riding the Paint.

Being older than my brother, I assured him I was a great cowpoke and could ride any horse I could put a saddle on.

The Paint stood still when I put the saddle blanket on, then shifted her weight when I put the saddle on her back. There was a little resistance putting the bridle in her mouth, but finally she accepted the bit in her mouth.

I led the horse out of the corral, put my foot in the stirrup, and hoisted myself into the saddle. Without warning, the Paint threw me into the air and off her back. I hit my head on a corral log on my way down to the ground.

The fall resulted in a concussion and a dislocated shoulder from when I hit the corral log.

I woke up in a small hospital with a serious head ache and my arm in a sling tied around my chest.

When I was released from the hospital, the doctor told me to be very careful and avoid any head injuries for at least a year.

#2

When summer ended, I started my freshman year of high school. I felt fine and wanted to play football for the school. My brother and I usually rode the school bus home after school. I told my brother to tell Mom and Dad that I was going to stay for football practice but would catch a ride home with our neighbor.

I got dressed in my football gear, eagerly awaiting the start of practice. We met in the gym where the coach explained what he expected from us and how hard we were going to work.

Unbeknownst to me, Mom picked up my brother at the first place the bus stopped. When he told her I had stayed for football practice, she immediately drove to the school.

I was standing in one of three lines, getting ready to begin exercising. Mom got out of the car and walked up to me, grabbed the helmet out of my hand, spun me around, and kicked my butt.

"Take that football stuff off and go get in the car," she said loudly.

The next few weeks in school were pure hell.

#3

My freshman year in college, I saw a girl I really wanted to date. Her family lived in the college town and her father was a local police officer.

When I found out the girl's name, I approached her, called her by name, and began to talk to her. I asked her for a date, and she accepted.

I bragged to one of my classmates about what a smooth operator I was.

85

"Be careful; her father is a local police officer and very protective of her," my classmate told me.

The night of the date, I knocked on the door to her house. My knock was answered by her father, who invited me into the house.

"Judy will be down in a few minutes, so I will lay out the rules for dating her," her father said. "Very simple: Whatever you do to my daughter, I will do to you."

Our date went very well, and I dated her a few more times. While walking her to her door, we were holding hands. Her father opened the door and said, "Okay, my turn." He grabbed my hand and walked slowly around the entire block, swinging my arm as we walked.

She apologized to me the next day and said she would understand if I didn't ask her for another date.

It wasn't a hard decision to make!

Winter Morning
Travis Dover

Awakening, the chill morning caresses my face and chest as I sit up from bed. I push the covers aside. My wife sleeps with my son beside her. He snores, being an inheritor of my poor sinuses. I pull the cover up over his chest only slightly. Sliding my feet into my shoes, I stand and stretch, then throw on my shirt. I step gingerly toward the bedroom door, avoiding the area that cries loudly when stepped upon. I make it out of the room and down the hall toward the stairs. My eldest daughter sleeps on a futon in the loft—she is a huddled, quilted pile; only her feet are visible hanging out one side.

As I walk down the stairs, I pause halfway and peer upward to a set of windows toward a sky that isn't as black as it was fifteen minutes ago. It reminds me of the sea's abyss. My mind wanders a minute through images of childhood, and I imagine a moon somewhere with a face, a locomotive pulling train cars over the stars and bursting through the high clouds. Somewhere an old man smokes a pipe. His wife mends a garment. Bacon is fried, dogs bark, Santa Clause and other childhood fancies go here and there on their missions. I breathe in deeply. My eyes come back to me from the stars and distant puff of cloud, from the glow of an out-of-sight moon, back into my window, to my house, and I wonder how my stocks are trading in premarket hours.

Downstairs, I turn on a dim yellow light and fix myself a double shot of espresso as quietly as one can. When done, I find my book on the counter where I had left it the night before and fall into my favorite recliner. I read a few lines before my mind wanders again. I stare up at a nearby wall that houses a small shelf of books adjacent to a crucifix. The crucifix was handmade in the Holy Land and has different soils and stones in the four ends—top, bottom, left and right. I meditate a moment on the Holy Land, and wonder if the dirt Jesus had stepped upon two thousand years ago is still there somewhere, maybe stuck to someone's shoe. Then, in my mind's eye, I watch as the war unfolds between Israel and Hamas. I recall the horrific things the terrorists did to innocent people on October 7th, 2023. Then, I watch as bombs tear apart an entire city, and another, buildings falling down on children in Gaza. The humanitarian efforts, the fighting, the depravity.

I stare down at my book and sip at my espresso. I had added more water to it to make an Americano—a fancy word for espresso mixed with water. It's cold down here, I think. Heat rises. I'm happy to be in my sweatpants. I sip from the warm cup again and am thankful for this dimly lit room, the book, the mug of brew, and a cold winter's morning. Lent begins soon, and I am happy to suffer a little, while so many suffer so greatly. I won't be going without my home or murdered family and friends—I won't be starving. I think this is my favorite time of year: February. Short days make for longer darkness, cold air, more time with the kids, an excuse to stay indoors and read, think, and enjoy a cup of coffee.

I haven't read three lines, and now I see a couple kids stalking down the stairs. More will soon follow. There are seven of them, after all. A board cries above me from someone's weight. My wife is awake. I set the coffee and book aside to be off to another favorite thing to do on these early February mornings, and that is making pancakes for my kids. I make myself another cup of espresso first. I'll need it.

Imposing Self-Freedom
Richard Weaver

As a product of the greatest generation, I was an active part
of many societal reforms and evolutions. Some of the changes were
the movie-making industry and social norms. The weekly movies
were preceded by a short "Serial" vignette of a hero tormenting and
chasing bad people. The end of the vignette leaves the hero on the
verge of certain demise. Usually, the cowboy hero was captured by
the Indians or his cattle were being stampeded and he would be in
the path of the charging animals. Or he was in the jungle and a lion
was about to eat him.

After the terrifying, suspenseful end of the serial episode the
main feature would begin, leaving the moviegoer wanting to return
the next week to see if the hero would live through his peril. Most of
the movies I saw in the late 1940s were made in black and white.

The main feature was filled with actors we all recognized and
admired, either for the manly role or, in the case of the actress, for her
beauty. All the heroes, including the females, smoked cigarettes, and
I was of the opinion that in order to be tough, I had to smoke
cigarettes. In my preteen years I, of course, could not smoke.
However, candy cigarettes were sold for a nickel a package and
substituted for real cigarettes in the world of my friends and me.

The movies evolved to Technicolor and more realistic plots
and the serials went the way of the Dodo Bird. During this
evolutionary state for movies, the actor still portrayed smoking as a
façade of strength, individualism and rebellion. It was not unusual to
sit in a movie theater that had ash trays in the arm rest of the seat and
was filled with cigarette smoke.

In my mid-teen years, I became interested in athletics and
played sports in junior high and high school. Our coaches forbade us
from smoking and would kick you off the team if you were caught
smoking or with cigarettes. Because of the smoking restrictions
administered by the coaches, I didn't smoke during my high school
years. It was still socially acceptable for people to smoke in public
buildings and public gatherings, however.

I enlisted in the army and found a freedom from the all the social restrictions of my teen years and home. I tried smoking in basic training and found it quite distasteful. Thinking I was going to take up smoking, I bought a carton of cigarettes at the PX and kept them in my foot locker. The first three weeks of basic training, I smoked four cigarettes, mostly to show other soldiers I was tough.

I took the carton of cigarettes on our first bivouac, thinking I was going to smoke them. As fate would have it, I was offered three dollars for a package of cigarettes. I decided not to smoke, but instead to sell the packages of cigarettes for five dollars.

I eventually began to smoke on a regular basis and became addicted, smoking a package a day. I became a regular smoker through my enlistment and into college. Smoking was still a socially acceptable habit and I didn't realize how addicted I had become to the nicotine.

When I entered my law enforcement career, smoking was still the "tough guy" standard, and I continued to smoke cigarettes.

The true effects of cigarette smoke on our health became more and more evident through science and health-related realities. I decided to quit.

I tried every advertised crutch to help stop smoking but they were all to no avail. The only statistic that had an impact on my thinking was the tar left in your lungs. According to the information, tar in the lungs has a ten-year half-life and it is the same tar used to pave a road. Although attention-getting, it still did not instill in me a strong desire to stop smoking.

The event that triggered my will power occurred when I was working court security for judges. A judge had been murdered during an escape attempt by an inmate from San Quentin Prison and triggered the need to have deputy sheriffs assigned to personal protection for the judges.

The incident occurred when I was twenty-five years old and assigned to three judges. I rotated between court rooms and walked the judges to their cars at the end of their work day.

One of the judges finished a jury trial and sequestered the jury. By law, a bailiff (deputy sheriff) was stationed outside the jury room and could not leave his post until the jury reached a verdict.

I was talking to a deputy who was sitting for the jury when the judge stepped out of his courtroom and told the deputy to go with him. We both told the judge of the legal requirement for the deputy to remain with the jury, but the judge insisted the deputy go with him while I stayed with the jury.

Thirty minutes later, I was sitting outside the jury room and had smoked the last cigarette I had. The need for a cigarette became overwhelming, but no remedy for my need was in sight.

Smoking in the courthouse was still legal and ash cans were provided in the halls. The cans were round with metal dished on top, half full of sand. When a smoker finished their cigarette, they would stick the lit end into the sand, leaving the unsmoked butt exposed.

I became so desperate for a cigarette that I began searching for a butt long enough for me to smoke. I picked one up and was about to put it into my mouth when I was struck by the thought, "Whose mouth last held the cigarette?"

The ashtray hunt triggered my thought process into realizing I HAD to quit smoking. For several days I struggled trying to find the mental path I needed to take that would end my addition to nicotine. One of my coworkers, who smoked three packages a day, quit. I asked him for the solution he used and he said, "Just don't smoke the next one."

I am sure if I had not overcome addiction and had not quit smoking, I would not have survived three heart attacks or colon cancer.

Doing My Job
Richard Weaver

Three deputy sheriffs and I were serving as range masters for the sheriff's office for which we worked. We converted the firearms training for the old "Camp Perry" training to survival shooting techniques. Camp Perry training is shooting at a stationary target. The targets were placed at eleven, fifteen, and twenty-five yards.

The survival training teaches a shooter to move between targets and fire two rounds in two seconds. The shooter is trained to look at the target, raise their weapon into their line of sight, and not use the sights to gain target acquisition.

As a favor to the undersheriff, I trained him in the survival techniques.

The undersheriff was impressed and his wife pressured him and the sheriff to start a survival class for women in the community.

I designed a class for shooting and weaponless defense specifically for women.

At the end of the three-week class, most of the students became proficient in survival shooting and a few in weaponless defense.

One of the women in the class was sitting at home in the late evening when a man burst through the front door of her house.

She kept a .357 Magnum in a box on the coffee table. She picked up the pistol and "double-tapped" two rounds into the center of the intruder's chest.

The local police department investigated the shooting and ruled it a self-defense shooting. The investigator described the entry wounds on the burglar as two wounds, less than an inch apart, in the center of the sternum.

Two days later I was at the patrol briefing and a deputy I had worked with several times sat near me. He looked as though he was near tears and upset.

I asked him why he was so somber.

"My brother was shot and killed in Millbrae a few nights ago. I know he was a dope fiend and a crook, but he was still my brother."

His statement still gives my conscience a twinge when I think about my part in the death of the intruder and the praise I received from the class members I taught.

Letter to Self
William Blaylock

Dear,

It has been a long time since I wrote; I suspect it's been over 30 years since we were last together. I hope you are well, and that you have had an enjoyable, rewarding life.

Back in 1987, I didn't even think about the year 2017, and now here it's transpired. Time continues, and we follow along with it, accomplishing who knew what. Now, here we are, April 2024.

You seemed to always be planning something, usually something to build. You wanted to build a small twelve-foot sailboat; you had plans for a home-built three-quarter scale P-51 airplane, and you wanted to hotrod your dad's old car. Were you able to complete any of those things? Did you restore that 1966 Ford Mustang? I remember you had big plans for that car. Plans like: custom interior, polished Magnesium wheels with street-legal racing slicks, metal flake candy-apple red paint, and a super-high-performance 427 engine. We sure enjoyed talking about and making plans for that car. I hope you have accomplished all your goals and dreams.

I never was what someone would call a forward-thinker. I did not plan too far into the future. I tend to act on, or react to, life at the time. I am not a believer in fate. No matter what you call it, serendipity, kismet, destiny, fortune, or luck, we can plan for this game of life. I do not mean to be flippant about it. That is not it at all; I simply prefer to accept life as it comes, be it wise or poor planning on my part. I have faith. Faith that all will work out in the end. I have faith in The Holy Trinity, and that faith provides me with what I need for a positive outlook. I have succumbed to changes in life and am prepared to continue.

I have had accomplishments in life. I am happily married to a good woman. Both my children are independent, productive members of society. Both ███████████ completed their college educations. They each paid off their school loans, and have good jobs. One, ███, is a construction inspector, and the other, ███, started and developed a successful flower and design business. As

94

you know, we all must take an occasional sidetrack. Sometimes we return to the mainline, and often we continue the new rail. I am proud of my children for how they have used their sidetracks.

Our granddaughter, ███████████████████, graduated from Cal State Santa Cruz, studying psychology and philosophy. I like to joke that she is going to philosophize whether there is, or is not, a psychology; or she may use it to evaluate me. While in college, she was able to study two semesters in Prague. During that time, she traveled, seeing many parts of France, Germany, Hungary, Denmark, Austria, and Italy. She is using her education to teach autistic children, and others who have learning and social disabilities. I am so very proud of her.

Our grandson, ████████████, is nine years old. They live in San Francisco, so we don't get to see him as much as we'd like, but I presume that's how all grandparents feel. He is polite, respectful, and accepting of everyone he meets. He cracks me up; he likes sushi and will try new things to eat. You might remember, our son always loved baseball, and still does, and so, as you can imagine, his son (our grandson) is playing Junior Giants Baseball. He is slender and can run fast. He is not as enthusiastic about it as his dad was, but he is only nine, and his interests and passions will continue to develop. He loves building anything he dreams up with Lego toys. He is amazing at it. He plays computer games with friends. They play from their respective homes simultaneously. (I don't understand how they do that.) He, and they, construct not only buildings, but entire cities, with creative amenities—I'm sure I wouldn't have thought of many of them. Absolutely awesome!

Another blessing is my ██████████ cancer is not advancing. It is not gone, but it hasn't changed either. The oncologist has extended exams to every twelve months after two years of every-four-and-six-months exams. We accept it as a gift from God.

I talk more about my family than myself, and that's my intention.

Until I write again, Peace and goodwill. Welcome home Brother.

Self

A Social Experiment
Richard Weaver

My enlistment in the Army ended after a three-year commitment. I enjoyed my enlistment but I learned after six months in the Army that I didn't want to be an enlisted soldier. I decided to finish college, take ROTC, and reenlist in the Army as an officer.

I enrolled in a Utah college carrying a fifteen-unit class schedule that included ROTC. My first semester went quite well and I found ROTC an easy class. My class included an old high school classmate, Bryan, from Idaho. I never associated with him in high school because each of us had other friends and interests.

Bryan was in his junior year of college but was still too young to buy alcohol. Because I was over 21, he asked me to buy some alcohol for him and his fraternity brothers. In Utah, at that time, the only place you could buy alcoholic beverages was in a "Glasshouse", which was a State-controlled liquor store. The store required the buyer to have a state-issued liquor permit to buy any booze.

I told Bryan I would not take the chance of buying liquor for a minor and risk going to jail over a bottle of booze. Bryan knew I loved sports and invited me to play for his fraternity's touch football team. I accepted his invitation and played several games for them.

The camaraderie with the team grew, and I became popular with them, not because I played football, but because I was old enough to buy booze. I was invited to the fraternity house for a party with the team and a sorority. I knew there was going to be booze at the party, so I took a pint of scotch with me.

The fraternity members were mostly rich kids and saw themselves as privileged and socially superior to other students. The party was a success, and I met several sorority sisters who showed some interest in me (I later learned their interest was that I could buy booze). I joined the fraternity and went through a hazing ritual that seemed very juvenile but was entertaining to the upper-classmen. I stood at the gym entrance and asked the spectators if they were waders or folders. The longer I associated with the fraternity, the more booze I consumed, just to make myself look more mature than the other brothers.

Some of the members were interested in getting a degree and then moving on with their lives. Others were only interested in the parties and the drinking. The habit of buying a pint of scotch every two weeks morphed into a pint a week, then one a day.

I became disgusted with myself and the snobbery of the fraternity brothers, but Bryan and I often talked about our high school years while sipping on a drink. When I finally realized I was in the clutches of alcohol and had to leave the environment that promoted my lifestyle, I told Bryan I was going to drop out of the fraternity. He put his drink on the table, walked away, and never spoke to me the rest of the semester.

I never reenlisted in the Army but instead chose a career in law enforcement. Twenty-five years later I returned to my hometown as the Chief of Police. After being sworn in as Chief of Police, I was invited to speak at a community service club which Bryan was a member of.

After the meeting, Bryan walked up to me and shook my hand. With tears in his eyes, he told me he was a recovering alcoholic and had been sober for five years. He told me he regretted not following my example of leaving the fraternity and taking charge of his life.

Although we are not good friends, I do admire him for finally taking charge of his weakness and living a clean and sober life.

Spelunking
Ralph Monterosa

It was a cool fall day as I walked through the entrance of the student center. I had just gotten out of my last class on a Friday afternoon. I was looking at a quiet weekend on a college campus that became a ghost town on weekends. Since finances were thin, Saturday had nothing to offer in the way of activities. Normally I would spend half the day at the ROTC indoor range. This Saturday, the range was closed. I might just have to spend the weekend at the library. Maybe I could find something going on in the student center? I was disappointed to find the place mostly empty.

There was glimmer of hope: sitting at a booth in the corner was Mike McKelvy, a fraternity brother and fellow ROTC Cadet. He had papers spread across the table. He was so involved with this exercise that he didn't see me sit down in front of him. I was there for a few minutes before he realized he was not alone. "Howdy Ralph, I didn't see you sit down. Been there long? I've been looking at this information to see where I might want to cave search this weekend. I think I might have enough information to get started."

Before he could continue, we were joined by Richard Christianson, another Cadet in the program. Richard was a local Texan, who was a quiet but always smiling friend. He was a big guy who had a difficult time moving around. He was unable to turn his head in either direction. To look left or right he would have to turn at the waist. I never thought to ask him about his problem. We continued to sit quietly watching Mike read his map and take notes as he went about his business.

Finally, he came up for air. Without being asked, he explained what he was doing. The information on the table looked like it might be a terrain map. Mike was a geology major. His plan after graduation was to attend the School of Mines in Golden, Colorado. It's fortunate for him to find something he had such a passion about. Mike never wasted words, and had a talent to get right to the point. "What are you two doing tomorrow?" Before we could answer, his next question was, "How would you like to look inside a cave, just down the road a piece."

Richard's response was my next thought: How far is just down the road a piece? (Especially in Texas.) Tell me more. Other than the location of the entrance, there wasn't much to tell. I don't remember saying yes, but Mike quickly added, "I'll pick you up in front of the student center at 1000 hours tomorrow." He was gone in the blink of an eye.

Richard added, "I guess we're going spelunking tomorrow." Since spelunking wasn't a New York City word, I only had a vague idea what we were doing. He asked if I had ever been in a cave befor. I had been on a boy scout trip to the caverns in Pennsylvania. I remember a large entrance, a wooden floor path, cathedral-size rooms that were well-lighted, and of course, a tour guide. Heck, there was nothing to it. Richard's response: "Good. I'll bring my camera."

When we met the next morning, I should have become suspicious. Richard and I were dressed very casual, like we were going to the corner drug store. On the other hand, Mike's get-up should have thrown up some red flags. He had on a pair of hiking boots, military fatigues, a canvas belt, and a jacket that looked much warmer than what we had on. He had on a flat-top fatigue hat. A large flash light was clipped to one side of his belt and a sheath knife to the other. We jumped in his jeep and were on our way. Mike drove for about an hour before we turned onto a gravel road. (So much for down the road a piece.) I know what it would be like to be in a good old Texas Rodeo. We then turned onto a dirt road which was a lot smoother.

He suddenly came to a stop and announced, "We're here." I looked around for a cave, but drew a blank. Good, no cave, let's go home. Mike pointed straight ahead. "There it is." I looked straight ahead and only saw a pile of large boulders. Richard asked, "Where's the cave?" That's it. "Where?" Under those rocks. "You sure?" Yes. Been out here before, but didn't go in. The entrance is under that pile.

This was the moment Richard and I were supposed to say, "No way. Let's go home." Mike assured us the earth science department had been inside and told him all about it.

We moved closer to this outcropping but I still didn't see anything that looked like a cave. As we got to the edge of the pile, Mike got down on all fours. "Look, here it is." Here's what? "The entrance to the cave." Richard and I got down as well. There was a space not tall enough to stand in. We would have to crawl under this large flat rock. It was about 30 feet wide, and maybe just as deep.

We could see a dark opening at the farthest point. Mike was halfway there as Richard crawled behind him. I was hesitantly keeping pace with Richard. As I looked to my right there was an open space with an invitation to crawl out. That would have been a better way to go. Just for an instant something seemed to move in that direction. Richard froze, as I almost climbed over him. Richard picked up a rock and flipped it that way. My chest began to pound. It was the unmistakable sound of a rattle snake. I almost climbed over him as we reached the entrance of the cave.

We could now stand up, with a two- or three-foot clearance. Mike was waiting for us. He had turned on his light, which lit up the cave as far as we could see. He opened his pack and handed one to each of us. We walked single file in a path that brought us deeper into a narrow passage. This was fine until the path made a few turns that made it feel like we were closing a door behind us. Mike said, Turn off your lights. We were dumb enough to comply! I've never been anywhere that had been that dark. Not the slightest bit of light. Not a good feeling.

My light went back on first. As I did, something moved on the ceiling, about a foot above my head. It was only about three inches long and as best I could tell had about 100 legs which moved faster than I could. Damn it. Why didn't I wear a hat.

I grabbed on to the back of Richard's shirt and wouldn't let go. In fact, I was pushing him along faster than he could move. I wasn't too fond of being last in the short parade. I couldn't see where we were going, and absolutely did not want to look back at where we had been. At times the floor would slant one way and then the other, making it difficult to keep our balance without reaching out for the wall. The ceiling would drop down, leaving very little headroom.

It was getting cold and damp as we tripped forward. We continued for about fifteen minutes. All of a sudden, the path widened into a large cavern with a large dome ceiling. In the center of the dome was a round hole where we could see daylight streaming in. There was a terrible, almost choking odor of ammonia. Mike jokingly said, "Watch this." He picked up a rock and tossed it up towards the ceiling. Just then, the ceiling began to move. Oh shit, hundreds of bats. Let's not wake them. Damn, why didn't I wear a hat.

Just then, Richard remembered his camera. He took a few quick pictures. I guess bats don't like to have their picture taken. We did an abrupt about face and started back the same way we had come. This time I climbed into second place. Richard had me by the collar and held on tight. Mike was too fast to hold onto. I made sure he was never more than a step ahead. Just as coming in, the walk was a constant up and down. That wasn't a problem until we hit a low spot, and we found ourselves standing in knee-deep water. I don't need to tell you what ran through my mind. I blocked all the rest of the what-ifs as best I could. You could imagine the relief as we turned a corner, and I could see a little glimmer of light.

Getting out actually seemed much shorter than the way we stumbled in. As we got out in a wider space, I took the lead. As we stepped out of the cave, I shook off any hitchhikers I may have picked up along the way. Richard said, "Good idea," and broke into some type of tribal dance. Mike was busy jotting down some notes, and was in no way affected by the trip. Just then, I remembered the welcoming committee we had on the way in. At this point, we didn't say anything. All communication was telepathic. We walked in long deliberate strides until we were back at the jeep. Mike tossed me the keys and told me to drive back to the student center.

Funny, but Richard and I never had any discussion about the experience. Whenever we were together, we would trade looks that would tell more than we could express. We sometimes shared a large grin. That said it all.

Since we were in military science (ROTC), we of course would have discussions about Viet Nam. We got to the point where we learned about the role of Tunnel Rats. These guys were special in

101

so many ways. It took far more courage than I could muster. P.S. I was barely five foot six and weighed 135 pounds. I'd take one in the foot before I would go in there.

Years later I would hear some bad news about Richard. The reason he couldn't turn his head was because he had tumors in his spine. They were cancerous and ultimately paralyzed him. He became a quadriplegic until it took his life.

To My Dear Friend Richard Christiansen, God bless you.

The Shower
Pete La Combe

One 30-day mission out of LZ Nancy, back in '69, seemed to be the itchiest of all. The bugs were at their peak—a buzz was in the air, you could say and see. Over there, there must have been a hundred different species of mosquitos, flies, ants, leeches, together with those blood-sucking earth worms and fleas—all in one place, among whom I was the favorite victim. If I got malaria, I figured it would be a ticket out of here at least (one better than lead poisoning from an AK-47). From head to toe, I had bites from giant horseflies. I would bet that they have elephant flies in Nam. Huge bumps, big bumps, little bumps. Some stung, then itched; some itched and burned later. At night the hum of mosquitos was annoying, loud, and constant. Even with a thick coat of mosquito repellent, we sweated it off in no time. I have seen them little FLICKERS bite me through a fresh thick coat of repellent and drown. Nobody was dumb enough to step on a trail of army ants, because in seconds, they could do more than make you itch: those bastards hurt. I was told they could skin you to the bone in no time—just thinking about it makes my bones itch. Tigers would run from those inch-long black devil ants, yielding to their king and queen, acknowledging that even in the jungle they have the right of way.

When we found out about the squawk boxes (radios mounted on jeeps), we were stopping at this LZ, and were invited to have hot showers, a hot meal, and to chill out for a bit before heading off. These showers were mounted to a white tile wall I had never seen in Nam, with at least 20 shower heads. They had the most pressure I have ever felt in my life; it was the best feeling ever. It was like a thousand fingers scratching every itch. As I rotated round and round, it was hard to believe how good it felt. I washed my dirt tan off; I was almost pink scrubbing off the sweat-soaked skin as the hot water blasted away. It was pure euphoria. I try to recreate that moment, except the itching part, to this day.

I stayed in the shower close to an hour. I was the very last one to get to the mess hall. I got my tray, put as much food on it as I could, smelled the air. I looked around the huge seating area. It must have housed 500 seats, all occupied except for one table with a vacant side. It was on the other side of the mess hall. As I walked up, I noticed one side had six Montagnard's solders (Aborigines) in loin cloths with arrows and crossbows, dressed like they came from the dawn of the second millennium, I thought. They were bobbing up and down on the lunch bench across from me as I looked down, grinning. The smell of the jungle on them was intense and pungent, radiating off them in waves. I never smelled anyone or anything like them before. The flies wouldn't get near them. Their jungle juice repellent must have worked better than ours. I sat down, looked up, and saw six smiling faces all chewing their bacon and eggs, mouths wide open, smacking their lips, gaping to show their half-chewed food to each other. It looked gross at first, but their exuberant enjoyment was, for them, a show of appreciation. It was contagious, the joy they were showing to me but not to anybody else. I started mimicking all six of them, all of us laughing our asses off, till we were stuffed. They said something to each other, rubbing their stomachs, passing gas, and smiling almost in unison when they looked at me. I was lucky: nobody in my squad liked lima beans, and my struggles to match their intake made all six grin. 'If you can't beat them, join them,'—made sense back then. I think that was their way of showing they enjoyed my company, as I did theirs. They blessed me that day with great memories, plus a lesson in ancient jungle etiquette taught by gnarly dudes with gnarly manners.

All Along the Watch Tower
Pete La Combe

I had about eight months in country when I passed on the job of motor squad driver for 39er, our three-quarter ton truck, handing it over to Johnson, our new FNG. He got the nickname "Poindexter" after he showed us a picture of him looking the part in his gold cap and gown in the graduation photo he had. Said he was summa cum laude. It was the first time I was in the back. I got to admit, that was a mistake. Sitting in a seat up front was more comfortable and I missed seeing where I going.

Bouncing down this dusty-ass, bumpy dirt road, swerving here and there, being thrown around the last five hours (eating dust) sucked. We were on a 500-vehicle convoy headed west, toward some mountaintop out in the jungle somewhere? Delta Troops' job was to return fire and keep the convoy moving. The trucks were huge along with their cargo, giant plows, as wide as the road. The convoy was so long you couldn't see the beginning or the end: it was everything needed to run a small town. Spanning the horizon, you could see the diesel smoke, mixed with a red dust cloud that floated like a huge snake disappearing into the blazing hot sun on one end and the cool green canopy on the other.

We were shattered throughout the convoy, offering support when needed. Tom left me his beat-up duct-taped cassette player and headphones. When he went back to the world, he said he'd get a brand-new boom box. He had it rigged up to use 6-volt batteries with alligator clips. I was trying to enjoy the day the best I could, sitting on sandbags in gear (goggles, bandana, steel pot and head phones blasting my ears). Choking on dust, kicked by the many tires, I was listening to the Jimi Hendrix Experience. "All Along the Watch Tower" was on, so I turned it up loud as hell, when the right front tire, then the rear, bounced with an explosion I didn't hear but felt. As I hung on to my M-16 and returned fire, the mortar rounds landing all around, we drove through it all. We had orders not to stop even under fire and to keep the trucks moving. We did. A few got hit, which we either went around or pushed out of the way. D Troop moved with the convoy, making sure nobody was left behind.

Medics cared for and medevacked the wounded, picking up anybody that needed a ride to the soon-to-be mountaintop firebase.

Every time I hear "All Along the Watch Tower" by Jimi, and especially the part where he sings, "The wind began to howl," I think of the time when the howling incoming mortars crashed around us, tipping us up onto two wheels as we drove through an explosive, dirt-filled dust cloud.

Boy & Dog
William Blaylock

A resting dog lay near a front tire of the truck left parked in the same spot for over a week. Clean on the outside, apparent from the sunlight reflecting off the driver's side. The young boy standing nearby wiped down and dusted the truck daily. His job was to keep the vehicle clean and ready to go whenever the driver wanted it. The truck, being parked under a leafy tree, made the boy's job troublesome, but it was his job. While the leaves were a nuisance to clean, the tree provided an arcadian, peaceful place to work. The owner had equipped it for rough terrain. It had a high-rise suspension, a heavy-duty push bar and high-intensity floodlights mounted in front of the grill.

The boy's friend, a mixed breed, more shepherd than any other, stays near to him. They have been together for two years. The boy found the dog as a pup, lying in tall grass, crying. He picked up the young pup, and name him Dog. The two made an instant connection. They were both rejections. No parents. No friends. No one who cared. They were alone together.

A Tennessee farmer saw the pair walking slow. They were shuffling along the hushed, dry, dusty, seldom-traveled dirt road, a mere forty yards from the front of his home. Near the road, the smell of dry dirt sifts through Boy's nostrils. However, close to the house, the air smells of damp, green, freshly-mowed grass. The farmer who lived there with his wife talked to the boy, who told him their story of wandering and no place to live. That was a good day for Boy and Dog. The farmer gave them shelter in his barn. Blankets and daily food and water. Everything the two friends needed.

Boy doesn't know how big the farm is. Once, when looking for Mister, who was discing a field, he followed the sound of the not-so-old Allison Chalmers tractor. It billowed and belched black smoke from the exhaust. Its attached equipment squealed and cried as steel rubbed against steel. Boy and Dog walked from when the sun was high in the sky until it fell to a low angle. It felt like the farm went on forever. When he found Mister, they all got into the tractor. Together, they rode for an hour, returning to the barn.

On the north-east edge of the farm lay a large lake. Boy and Dog frequented the lake to fish and explore. Its ground-fed, beautiful, blue, crisp water was enticing, beckoning for Boy and Dog to wade and swim. Boy enjoyed the fresh smell of the clean water and they went there often. Together, they fished from the bank, using an old bamboo pole given to them by their friend, Mister Farmer. It didn't have a new fancy reel with line, sinkers, and bobber; only ten feet of fishing line tied to the end of the pole with an old rusty steel hook on the end to snare a worm.

One day, while at the lake, Boy sees a magnificent black horse heading toward them. The horse was more than black. Shiny, it looked like it had deep blue mixed with its raven-black coat, sophisticated long flowing main and tail trailing behind with pride. It ran along the edge of the water. As the mare passed, Boy sees and hears the water splashing up from her hooves. Dog shows interest and gave a brief effort to, not so much chase, but follow the wondrous creature.

Life is good for Boy and Dog.

.

Made in the USA
Columbia, SC
12 November 2024

46016880R00065